The Rat-a-Tat
Mystery

The Rat-a-Tat Mystery

ENID BLYTON

Illustrated by Eric Rowe

AWARD PUBLICATIONS LIMITED

For further information on Enid Blyton
please contact www.blyton.com

ISBN 1-84135-172-5

Text copyright The Enid Blyton Company
Illustrations copyright © 2003 Award Publications Limited

Enid Blyton's signature is a trademark of
The Enid Blyton Company

This edition published by permission of
The Enid Blyton Company

First published 1951 by William Collins Sons & Co. Ltd
This edition first published 2003

Published by Award Publications Limited,
27 Longford Street, London NW1 3DZ

Printed in India

CONTENTS

1

Christmas Holidays

"How long do these Christmas holidays last?" said Mr Lynton, putting his newspaper down as a loud crash came from upstairs. "I sometimes think I'm living in a madhouse – what *are* those children doing upstairs? Are they practising high jumps or something?"

"I expect it's Snubby, as usual," said Mrs Lynton. "He's supposed to be making his bed. Oh, dear – there he goes again!"

She went to the door and called up the stairs. "Snubby! What in the world are you doing? You are making your uncle very angry."

"Oh, sorry!" shouted back Snubby. "I was only moving things round a bit and the dressing-table fell over. I forgot you were underneath. Hey, look out – Loony's coming down the stairs, and he's a bit mad this morning."

A black spaniel came hurtling down the stairs at top speed and Mrs Lynton hurriedly got out of the way. Loony slid all the way along the hall and in at the sitting-room door, almost to Mr Lynton's feet. He was most surprised to receive a smart slap on the head from Mr Lynton's folded newspaper. He shot out of the door almost as fast as he had come in.

"What a house!" groaned Mr Lynton as his wife came back. "As soon as Snubby arrives peace and quiet vanish. He makes Diana and Roger three times as bad, too – as for that dog Loony, he's even more of a lunatic than usual."

"Never mind, dear. After all, Christmas only comes once a year," said Mrs Lynton. "And poor old Snubby must have somewhere to go in the holidays – you forget he has no father or mother."

"Well, I wish he wasn't *my* nephew," said Mr Lynton. "And why must we have his dog Loony every time we have Snubby?"

"Oh, Richard, you know Snubby wouldn't come here if we didn't have Loony – he adores Loony," said his wife.

"Ha!" said Mr Lynton, opening his newspaper again. "So Snubby won't go anywhere without Loony – well, tell him next holidays we won't have that dog here; then perhaps Snubby won't inflict himself on us!"

"Oh, you don't really mean that, dear," said Mrs Lynton. "Snubby just gets on your nerves when you're home for a few days.

You'll be back at the office soon."

Upstairs, Snubby was sitting on his unmade bed, talking to his cousins, Diana and Roger, and fondling Loony's long silky ears. They had come to see what the terrific crashes were.

"You'll get into a row with Dad," said Roger. "You never will remember that your room is over the sitting-room. Whatever do you want to go and lug the furniture about for?"

"Well, I didn't really mean to move it," said Snubby. "But a pound went under the chest-of-drawers, and when I moved it out I thought it would look better where the dressing-table is, but the beastly thing went over with a crash."

"You're going to get a good telling-off from Dad pretty soon," said Diana. "I heard him say you were working up for one. You really are an ass, Snubby. Dad goes back to the office soon. Why can't you behave till then?"

"I do behave!" said Snubby indignantly. "Anyway, who spilled the coffee all over the breakfast table this morning? Not me!"

Roger and Diana stared at their red haired, freckle-faced cousin, and he stared back at them out of his green eyes. They were both fond of the irrepressible Snubby, but, really, he could be very irritating at times. Diana gave an impatient exclamation.

"Well, I don't wonder Dad gets tired of you, Snubby! You and Loony rush about the house like a hurricane – and why can't you teach Loony to stop taking shoes and brushes from people's bedrooms? Did you know he's taken Dad's clothesbrush this morning? Goodness knows how he got it off the dressing-table."

"Oh, golly! Has he really?" said Snubby, getting off the bed in a hurry. "There'll be another explosion from Uncle Richard when he discovers that. I'll go and find it."

Christmas had been a mad and merry time in the Lyntons' house. All the children had come home from school in high spirits, looking forward to plenty of good food, presents and fun. Snubby had been a little subdued at first, because he was afraid that his school report might be even worse than usual, and his uncle and aunt had been pleasantly surprised to find him most polite and helpful.

But this wore off after a few days, and Snubby had now become his usual riotous, ridiculous self, aided in every way by his black spaniel, Loony. His uncle had quickly become very tired of him, especially since Snubby had forgotten to turn off the tap in the bathroom and flooded the floor. If it hadn't been Christmas time Snubby would certainly have got a first-class telling-off!

All the same, everyone had enjoyed

Christmas, though the children wished there had been snow.

"It doesn't seem like Christmas without snow," complained Snubby.

"Oh, we'll get plenty as soon as Christmas is gone," said Mrs Lynton. "We always do. Then you can go out the whole day long, and snowball and toboggan and skate – and I shall be rid of you for a little while!"

But there had been no snow yet, only a drizzling rain that kept the children indoors for most of the time, much to Mr Lynton's annoyance. "Why must they always talk at the tops of their voices?" he said in exasperation. "And is there any need to have the radio on so loudly? And will someone tell that dog Loony that if I fall over him again he can go and live out-of-doors in the shed?"

But it really wasn't any good telling Loony things like that. If he wanted to sit down and scratch himself, he sat down, no matter whether someone was coming along to trip over him or not. Even Snubby couldn't make him stop. Loony just looked up with his melting spaniel eyes, thumped his little tail and then went on scratching.

"I don't know why you scratch!" said Snubby, in exasperation. "Pretending you've got fleas! You know you haven't, Loony. Oh, get up, do!"

One rainy morning Diana was moping about, getting in her busy mother's way. "Oh, Diana, dear, do get something to do!" said Mrs Lynton. "Have you done all your morning jobs – made your bed, dusted your room, done the—"

"Yes, Mummy – everything," said Diana. "I really have. Do you want me to help you?"

"Well, will you take down all the Christmas cards?" said her mother. "It's time they were down. Stack them neatly in a big cardboard box, so that we can send them to Aunt Lucy – she makes them into new cards to sell for her children's charity."

"Right!" said Diana. "Oh, there's Snubby with his mouth-organ. Mummy, doesn't he play it well?"

"No, he doesn't," said her mother. "He makes a simply horrible noise with it. Let him do the cards with you, then perhaps he'll put it down and forget it. I really do believe your father will go mad if Snubby wanders round the house playing it."

"Snubby, come and help with the Christmas cards," called Diana. "Look out, Mum – Loony's coming down the stairs."

"Christmas cards? What do you mean?" said Snubby, coming into the room. "Oh – take them down? Okay! It's always fun to look at them again. Let's put all the funny ones into a pile."

He and Diana were soon happily taking down the colourful cards. They read each one and laughed at the funny ones, stacking them neatly into a box.

"Oh, here's the one Barney sent us!" said Diana. "Look – isn't it marvellous! Just like old Barney too."

She held up a big card, on the front of which was a picture of a fairground. Drawn neatly in one corner was a boy with a monkey on his shoulder.

"Barney's drawn himself and Miranda on the card," said Diana. "Snubby, I wonder how he enjoyed Christmas-time with his family for the very first time in his life!"

Roger came into the room just then, and picked up Barney's card too. "Good old Barney!" he said. "I wish we could see him these hols. I say – wasn't it marvellous how he found his father and discovered that he had a whole family of his own?"

"Yes," said Diana, remembering. "He spent all his life in a circus with his mother, and thought his father was dead. And when his mother died, she told him his father was still alive, and he must find him . . ."

"And he went out to look for his father, and hunted everywhere," said Roger. "And then at last he met him last hols, at that dear little seaside place where we were staying – and what an awfully nice man he was, exactly like Barney . . ."

"Oh, yes," said Diana, remembering it all clearly. "And then dear old Barney discovered that he hadn't only a father, but a grandfather and grandmother and an uncle and aunts . . ."

"And cousins!" finished Snubby. "Gosh, what a wonderful Christmas Barney must have had. I bet he's forgotten about us now!"

"I bet he hasn't!" said Diana at once. "I say – I've got a smashing idea! Let's ask Mummy if we can have Barney to stay for a few days! Then we'll hear all his news."

"And we'll see Miranda again," said Snubby, thrilled. Miranda was Barney's pet monkey. "Do you hear that, Loony? We'll see Miranda!"

"Come on – let's go and ask Mummy this very minute!" said Diana, and flew out of the room. "Mum! Mum! Where are you?"

2

Barney

The three children raced upstairs to find Mrs Lynton. Loony was with them, almost tripping them up, he was so anxious to get to the top of the stairs first. He barked as he went, sensing the children's excitement and wanting to join in.

Mr Lynton, trying to write letters in his study, groaned loudly. "That dog! I really will have him kept out of doors if he goes on like this!"

"Mummy! We've got such a good idea!" said Diana, finding her mother putting clean towels into the bathroom.

"Have you, dear?" said her mother. "Snubby, could you tell me how you get your towel as black as this? You haven't been climbing chimneys by any chance, have you?"

"Ha-ha! Funny joke!" said Snubby, politely.

"Oh, Mummy, do listen. We've got a splendid idea!" said Diana again.

"Yes! Can we have Barney to stay for a few days, Mum?" said Roger, going straight to the point. "Do say yes! You like Barney, don't you?"

"And we haven't seen him since the summer holidays," said Diana. "Not since he found his father and all his new family, and went to live with them."

"And we simply must see him," said Snubby, snatching the bathmat away from Loony, who was shaking it as if it were a rat.

"Well, dears," began Mrs Lynton, looking most uncertain. "Well . . . I really don't know what to say."

"Oh, why? Why can't we ask Barney – and Miranda too, of course?" said Diana, astonished. "You always liked him, Mummy, you know you did."

"Yes, dear, and I do still," said her mother. "But I don't feel that Daddy will welcome anyone else here while you three are turning the house upside-down, and—"

"Oh, we don't turn it upside down!" cried Diana. "Haven't I been tidying things all the morning? Oh, Mummy, we'll be as quiet and tidy as anything if you'll let Barney come. We simply must hear his news before we go back to school again."

"Well, you must ask your father, Diana," said her mother. "If he says yes, Barney can certainly come. I'll leave it entirely to him."

"Oh," said Diana, looking gloomy.

"Please can't you ask him, Mummy?"

"No," said her mother. "Stop turning on the taps, Snubby. I said *stop*. And take Loony out of the bathroom, please. He'll have that sponge next, out of the bath rack."

"Come on, Loony," said Snubby, in a sorrowful voice. "We're not wanted here. We'll go and have a game together in the garage."

"No, you won't," said Roger firmly. "You'll come and back us up when we ask Dad if we can have Barney."

"I can't," said Snubby. "Uncle said he didn't want to set eyes on me again this morning. Or Loony either."

"Oh, well – you come, Di, and we'll tackle Dad together," said Roger. "And for goodness sake, Snubby, don't start playing your mouth-organ outside the study door just when we're inside."

Loony shot down the stairs at top speed as usual, followed by Snubby three steps at a time. Mrs Lynton shook her head and smiled to herself – nobody, nobody would ever teach Snubby and Loony not to hurl themselves downstairs.

Mr Lynton heard a discreet knock on his study door and raised his head from his letters. "Come in!" he said, and in came Diana and Roger.

"What it it?" asked their father. "Surely you don't want any pocket money yet, after all the money you had given to you at Christmas?"

"No, Dad, no," said Roger hurriedly. "We shouldn't dream of asking you for any yet. Er – we just wondered if – er – well, we thought it would be nice if—"

"Nice, and kind too," said Diana. "If we – er – if Barney could—"

"What is all this?" said her father impatiently. "Can't you ask a straight question?"

"Well, we wondered if Barney could come to stay for a few days," said Diana, bringing it all out in a rush. "You remember Barney don't you, Dad? The circus-boy we got to know so well."

"Yes, I remember him," said Mr Lynton. "Nice boy – very blue eyes – and didn't he have a monkey?"

"Yes, Dad!" said Roger eagerly. "Miranda – a perfect darling. Could we have them to stay?"

"Ask your mother," said his father.

"We have," said Roger, "and she says we're to ask you."

"Then I say no," said Mr Lynton firmly. "And I'm pretty certain your mother really wants to say no as well – you're all wearing her out these holidays! Also, we've got your Great-uncle Robert coming for three days, and I've really been wondering if I can't send Snubby and Loony off to Aunt Alice while Uncle Robert is here – I don't feel that the old gentleman will be able to cope with the three of you and that mad dog Loony too."

"Oh, Dad! You didn't ask Great-uncle in the Christmas holidays, surely!" cried Diana. "He talks and talks and talks, and we daren't say a word, and—"

"Perhaps that's why I asked him!" said her father, a sudden twinkle in his eye. "No – actually the old fellow asked himself. He hasn't been well, which is why I'm sure he can't cope with Snubby and Loony – and the mouth-organ."

"Oh," said Diana sadly. "Well, it's no good asking Barney then – there wouldn't be room, for one thing. Oh, and I did so want to see him these hols and now we shan't see him for ages. Couldn't we possibly put Great-uncle off, Dad?"

"No, we couldn't," said her father. "And even if we did, I wouldn't have Barney here – one more to add to the madhouse! And you might warn Snubby he may have to go to his Aunt Alice's soon."

Snubby was horrified at this news. "But I don't like being there!" he said. "Loony has to live in a kennel – and I have to wash at least twenty times a day! I say, I won't play my mouth-organ any more. And I'll stop whistling. And I'll tiptoe down the stairs, and—"

"Ass!" said Roger. "That would only

make Mum think you were ill, or sickening for something! Blast! All our plans made for nothing!"

"And we shan't see Barney now," said Diana. "Or that darling little Miranda."

"I say," said Snubby suddenly. "Look – it's snowing!"

They ran to the window and looked out. Yes, big snowflakes were falling steadily down. Diana looked up at the sky, but the snowflakes were already so thick that they hid it completely.

"If it goes on like this, we'll have some fun," said Roger, feeling more cheerful. "And when Great-uncle comes to stay we can keep out of his way all day long – we'll be out in the snow, tobogganing!"

"And skating, if there's any ice," said Diana, thrilled.

"But I shan't be here!" said Snubby, in such a desperate voice that the others laughed. "I shall be with my Aunt Alice and Uncle Henry, with poor old Loony howling by himself out in his kennel."

"Poor Snubby. Never mind. Perhaps Great-uncle won't come," said Diana.

But the next day there was a letter from Great-uncle announcing that he was arriving in two days' time. Snubby looked at his aunt in despair. Would he be sent away? He was ready to promise anything rather than that. Especially as the snow was now beautifully thick and deep, and the ponds had begun to freeze. There would be no tobogganing or skating at his Aunt Alice's, he knew that.

But Mrs Lynton was quite firm. If Great-Uncle Robert was not very well, then the worst thing in the world for him would be a dose of Snubby and Loony. He might even have a heart attack at some of the things Loony did.

"I must phone to your Aunt Alice at once," she said. "Don't look like that, Snubby – the world isn't coming to an end."

She went into the hall to phone – and almost as she touched the receiver, the shrill bell rang out.

"I hope it's to say Great-uncle can't come!" cried Snubby. But it wasn't. Mrs Lynton turned round, smiling. "Who do you think wants to speak to you?" she said. "It's Barney!"

"Barney!" cried everyone, and they all rushed to the telephone. Roger grabbed the receiver first. "Barney! Is it really you? Did you have a good Christmas?"

Then he listened to Barney's reply – and suddenly a look of utter delight came over his face. "Oh, Barney! What a wonderful idea! Yes, I'll ask Mum – hold on, I'll ask her straight away!"

Snubby and Diana could hardly wait for Roger to ask his mother whatever it was that Barney wanted to know.

"Mum!" said Roger, "Barney and one of his cousins are going to stay at a house his grandmother owns, by a little lake surrounded by hills – the lake is frozen and the hills are covered with snow so there will be tobogganing and skating. And he says can we go too?"

There were shrieks of delight from Diana and Snubby. "Of course we'll go, of course!"

"Barney says if you say yes, his grandmother will phone you to make all the arrangements," said Roger, his eyes shining. "Oh, Mum – it's all right, isn't it? We can go to stay with Barney, instead of him coming here, and Snubby won't have to go to his Aunt Alice's – and Great-uncle Robert can come here in peace, without any of us to worry him. Oh, Mum – we can go, can't we?"

3

An Exciting Invitation

Mrs Lynton looked at the three eager children, and nodded her head, smiling round at them.

"Yes, I don't see why you shouldn't. In fact, I think it's an excellent way of solving our difficulties. Oh, Snubby, dear, don't!"

Snubby caught hold of his aunt and was waltzing her round and round in delight, shouting, "Hip-hip-hip, hooray, it's a hap-hap-happy day!"

Mr Lynton came out into the hall in surprise, and was told what the excitement was about. He listened with approval.

"Ha! That will give your great-uncle a little peace and quiet – and us too," he said. "I hope you're not going to leave Loony behind. I really should like to see the back of that dog for a little while."

"You will, you will!" shouted Snubby, approaching his uncle to give him a waltz-round too, he was so very relieved. But fortunately he thought better of this – his uncle did not take kindly to such idiotic manners.

Roger was already telling Barney of his parents' consent, and getting a few more details. Diana snatched the receiver from him after a minute or two, longing to have a word with dear old Barney. A little chattering noise greeted her.

"Oh, is that you, Miranda!" she cried, enchanted to hear the familiar monkey-chatter once more. "We'll be seeing you soon, Miranda, soon, soon, soon."

"Woof!" said Loony, not understanding what was going on at all, and quite amazed at all the excitement. He tried to tug the mat from under Mr Lynton's feet and run off with it, but Snubby stopped him just in time.

Everyone was thrilled to hear from Barney. After Snubby had had a few words on the phone with him too, the receiver was put down and they all trooped into the sitting-room to talk over the exciting news.

"Fancy – a house in the middle of snowy hills and by a frozen lake too, it couldn't be better!" said Roger exultantly. "I must look out my skates. You're lucky, Snubby, you had new ones for Christmas."

"What about our toboggan?" said Diana. "I don't believe it's any good for us now – too small. We haven't used it for about three years!"

"I'll buy a new one with my Christmas

money," boasted Snubby. "Oh, I say – I wish I could buy skates for Loony!"

Roger laughed. "I wish you could. Loony would look priceless on skates – he wouldn't know which skate to use first!"

"Oh, it's too good to be true!" said Diana, sinking into a chair. "Mummy, you don't mind us going, do you? You won't be lonely, will you?"

"Dear me, no," said her mother. "I shall be glad to have time to devote to your great-uncle. Thank goodness Loony won't be here. When is Barney's grandmother going to telephone about the day and time and other arrangements, Roger? Did Barney say?"

"Yes, she'll phone tonight," said Roger. He turned to the others. "Barney sounded exactly the same, didn't he?" he said.

"Exactly," agreed the others.

"But why shouldn't he?" said Mrs Lynton, surprised.

"Oh, I don't know," said Roger. "After being a circus-boy so long – with worn-out clothes and often hardly enough to eat – and then finding a whole new family, and having to have lessons and decent clothes and table meals instead of camping out – well, somehow I thought he might have changed."

"Barney will never change," said Snubby. "Never. I say, think of tobogganing down steep hills – whooooosh!" He slid at top speed over the polished floor, and stopped when he saw his aunt's face. "And skating round and round – and in and out—"

He skated into a little table and Diana just caught it as it fell. "Don't be more of an idiot than you can help!" she said. "I bet you'll fall down a thousand times before you can skate even half a dozen steps. Ha – I'm looking forward to seeing you sitting down with a bump on the ice!"

Barney's grandmother phoned to Mrs Lynton that evening. She had a kind, very soft voice, and Mrs Lynton thought how lucky Barney was to have a grandmother who sounded so nice. She told the waiting children what the old lady had arranged.

"She says that this house in the hills has been shut up for some time," said Mrs Lynton. "Her sons and daughters used to use it for winter sports when they were young. She is sending someone to clean it up and air it, and it should be ready for you to go in two days' time."

"Is any adult going with them?" asked Mr Lynton. "They must have someone sensible there."

"Barney's very sensible," said Snubby, at once.

"Mrs Martin, that's Barney's grandmother, says she has asked her daily help's sister to look after them," said Mrs Lynton. "She will cook for them and dry their clothes, and see that they don't do anything too idiotic. But I hope Roger will see to that, as well. He's quite old enough to take charge, with Barney."

"We'll be all right," said Roger. "You needn't worry, Mum. My word – only two days and we'll be down at this little house!"

"It doesn't sound very little," said his mother. "There are five or six bedrooms, and a big old kitchen, and two or three other rooms. You'll have to help to keep it tidy, or the daily's sister will walk off and leave you!"

"I'll help her," promised Diana. "And we can all make our beds – though all Snubby does is simply to get out of his in the morning and pull the sheets and blankets up again."

"Tell-tale," said Snubby at once. "It's my bed, isn't it?"

"I think tomorrow we'd better look into the question of skates and boots and clothes," said Mrs Lynton. "And you will all need good wellingtons, of course. I hope you brought yours back from school, Snubby. You forgot them last term."

"Yes, I brought them back. Anyhow, I quite well remember bringing one back," said Snubby, helpfully.

"What's the house called?" asked Diana.

"Well – I think I must have heard it

wrongly over the phone," said her mother, "but it sounded like Rat-a-Tat House."

Everyone laughed. "How lovely!" said Diana. "I hope that *is* its name. Rat-a-Tat House – why ever was it called that, I wonder?"

Next day was a busy one. Boots, socks, gloves, sweaters, skates – all were pulled out and carefully examined. The weather remained very cold and frosty, and snow fell again in the night. The forecast was cold weather, much snow, and hard frost – just right for winter sports, as Snubby kept announcing. He produced his mouth-organ once more, and nearly drove everyone mad by trying to learn a new tune. In the end, Mrs Lynton took it away and packed it at the very bottom of one of the suitcases that were going with them.

But, not to be outdone, Snubby then went about pretending to strum on a banjo, and made a peculiar twanging noise with his mouth half-closed as he strummed an imaginary banjo with his fingers and thumb. This was really worse than the mouth-organ, and unfortunately, as the banjo was purely imaginary, it could not be taken away from him.

"Can't that boy be sent to Rat-a-Tat House today?" demanded Mr Lynton, hearing the banjo passing his door for the twentieth time. "It's a good thing he won't be here when Great-uncle Robert comes."

At last the suitcases were all packed, the skates strung together, and the clothes set out fresh for the next morning, when they were to join Barney. Loony rushed around eagerly all the time, trying to help, and making off with shoes and bundles of socks whenever they were put ready to pack. Even

Snubby got a bit tired of him when he met Loony rushing up the stairs, just as he, Snubby, was rushing down, and both arrived in a bruised and tangled heap at the bottom.

"Ass of a dog!" said Snubby fiercely to the surprised Loony. "I'll leave you behind if you do that again. I nearly broke my leg. Grrr! Bad dog!"

Loony put his tail down and crept under the hall chest. There was a smell of mouse there and he had a wonderful time scrabbling round and round to find it, snuffling loudly all the time, much to Mr Lynton's amazement.

"We're going to Barney's home first, and then go on with him and his cousin to Rat-a-Tat House," said Roger to the others. "I wish tomorrow would come. I say – I wonder what the cousin's like. Mum, how long can we stay away?"

"Till the snow's gone, I should think," said his mother. "That's what Barney's grandmother said. But, of course, if it lasts more than a week or so, you'll have to come back because of getting ready for school again."

Roger groaned. "Don't mention the word again! Snubby, *stop* that noise. Or play another instrument for a change. That imaginary banjo of yours is getting boring."

Snubby obligingly changed over to a zither, which was certainly much pleasanter.

He really was a marvel at imitating sounds. Mrs Lynton hoped he wouldn't start on a drum next!

The morning came at last – a brilliant morning, with a clear blue sky and pale yellow sun, and the snow underfoot as crisp as sugar. "Heavenly!" said Diana. "Just exactly right for us!"

Off they went in a taxi to catch the train to Barney's town, Loony too, so excited that he had to be put on the lead. Now for a good time – now for some sport – hurrah for the winter holidays!

4

At Barney's House

Barney's home was at Little Wendleman, and a car was at Wendleman station to meet them – a nice estate car with plenty of room for luggage. Best of all, Barney was there to meet them, with Miranda sitting excitedly on his shoulder.

"Barney! Good old Barney! And Miranda; hey, Miranda!" shouted Snubby, hanging out of the compartment window as the train drew in. He opened the door and he and Loony fell out together. Barney ran up in delight, his brilliant blue eyes shining as brightly as ever. Miranda, the little monkey, leaped up and down on his shoulder and chattered at the top of her voice. She knew everyone immediately.

"Barney! Dear old Barney!" said Diana, and gave him a hug. Roger clapped him on the back, and Snubby grinned all over his freckled, snub-nosed face. As for Loony, he went completely mad, lay on his back, and did one of his bicycling acts at top speed, barking loudly all the while.

"Hello!" said Barney, his brown face glowing with pleasure at seeing his friends again. "Gosh – it's grand to see you all again. Isn't it, Miranda?"

The little monkey leaped on to Diana's shoulder and whispered in her ear, holding the lobe in her paw the way she often did. Diana laughed. "Darling Miranda – you haven't changed a bit, not a bit."

Barney looked different. He was no taller and no fatter, and his face was as brown as ever. But now he was dressed well and his hair was cut properly. In fact he looked extremely nice, and Diana gazed at him in admiration.

Barney laughed, as he saw the eyes of all three on him. "Do I look so different?" he said, in the voice they knew so well, with the slight American twang he had picked up in his circus travels. "I'm not a circus-boy any more but I'm still the same, see? I'm just Barney – aren't I, Miranda?"

Miranda leaped on to his shoulder again and jigged up and down, chattering in monkey-language. What did she care how Barney was dressed, or where he lived, or what he was? It was all the same to her. He was just Barney.

"Yes, you're still just Barney," said Diana, and gave a little sigh of relief. She had wondered just a little if having a family, and a nice house and money to spend, would have changed Barney – but no, it hadn't.

"Come on," said Barney. "The car's here, see, and there's my father driving it." He said the words "my father" in a very proud voice. Diana felt touched. How very, very glad Barney must be to have a father of his own, and to have found him after so many years of thinking he was dead!

Barney's father, Mr Martin, was sitting at the wheel of the car. The children marvelled at the likeness between the two – bright blue, wide-set eyes, corn-coloured hair, a wide mouth, ready to smile. Yes, they were certainly father and son. The only real difference between their faces was that Barney's was so much browner than his father's.

"Hello, kids!" said Mr Martin, and smiled, looking more like Barney than ever. "Nice of you to come all this way to see Barnabas – or Barney, as you call him. Hop in! We're to have lunch at his grandmother's, and then I'll take you to Rat-a-Tat House."

"Thank you very much, Mr Martin," said Roger politely. "It's good of you to meet us like this – and jolly good of Barney's grandmother to invite us to stay at Rat-a-Tat House. We're thrilled."

The boys piled the suitcases into the back. Loony clambered in, and sat up in a corner so that he could look out of the window.

He loved hanging his head out of a car, his long ears flapping in the breeze. He was delighted to see Barney again, though he wasn't so sure about Miranda the monkey. He had suddenly remembered how she used to ride on his back, jigging up and down in a most aggravating manner. He looked at her out of the corner of his eye. Would she try that old trick again?

The car drew up in the drive of a pleasant looking house, timbered, with white walls, tall chimneys and wide casement windows. As they drew up, the front door flew open, and a little old lady stood there, as brown-eyed as the monkey that sat on her shoulder.

"Ah, here you are!" she cried. "Welcome, welcome! I've longed to meet dear Barney's friends. Come along in, come along in!"

The children liked Barney's grandmother at once. She had curly white hair, a very pink soft-cheeked face, brown eyes, and a lively smile. They smiled to see the monkey on her shoulder as they shook hands.

"Ah – you see I have a monkey just like Barnabas!" she said in a merry, bird-like voice. "Monkeys run in our family – my mother kept two. Jinny, here are good friends!"

Jinny, the little monkey, held out a tiny, wizened paw in a very solemn manner and shook hands with each of them. Loony

stared in astonishment at her. What –
another monkey – or was he seeing double?

Soon they were all sitting in a cosy room,
with a blazing fire, bright curtains and a
lovely meal laid ready on a round table.
Snubby looked at it approvingly. Hot
tomato soup to begin with – now that was
just what he felt like! He took his place at
once and beamed round. This was the kind
of thing Snubby enjoyed.

"What comes next?" he asked Barney, in
a loud whisper.

"Ah – Barnabas has told me what you
like," said the old lady, who had very sharp
ears. "Sausages – plenty of them – and fried
onions and tomatoes, and potatoes and peas.
Barnabas has had many a meal with you, I

know, and now I am proud you should have a meal with him."

Snubby thought this sounded fine. What a nice old lady. Barney was certainly lucky to belong to such a splendid family. For a second Snubby was just a little jealous when he looked at Barney's handsome, smiling father. He would have liked a father like that – but he had no parents at all, worse luck. Snubby simply couldn't understand children who grumbled at their parents – they didn't know how lucky they were to have them!

It was a very pleasant meal. Barney told them all about the lessons he had had during the last term. He had left school early, and his father had thought he must have plenty of private coaching before he sent him anywhere. The boy was very intelligent, and enjoyed his lessons immensely.

"He's as good at them as he is at walking the tightrope or turning cartwheels!" said his father, with a laugh.

"How marvellous!" said Snubby, enviously. "I'm no good at either! Barney – do you ever miss the circuses and fairs and shows you used to belong to?"

"Sometimes," said Barney. "Not often. But just at times I think of what fun it was sleeping out under the stars or having a tasty meal out of some cook-pot in a fair when I was very hungry – and I miss the show people a bit."

"You can always go off for a taste of that life again, whenever you want to, Barney," said his father, smiling at him.

"I know," said Barney. "But I shall always come back home – come back here to you and Granny. I like the freedom of the show-life but I like putting out roots too, as I can here. That feeling of belonging somewhere, to a place or a family, that's what I've missed all my life, and now I've got it, I'm going to keep it."

The talk went on during the meal, happy, jolly talk, friendly and intimate. Loony lay beneath the table, amazed at the variety of titbits that came down to him from Snubby, Roger and Barney. Miranda, curious to see why Loony was so peaceful, slid down a table leg to investigate, and joined in Loony's little feast, much to his annoyance. Jinny, the other monkey, seldom left her mistress's shoulder, and gravely took little titbits in her tiny paw. Sometimes she patted the soft old cheek near to her, and often did what Miranda did to Barney – slid a small paw down her mistress's neck to warm her tiny fingers.

"Now, after lunch, the car will take you all to Rat-a-Tat House," said Barney's grandmother. "Mrs Tickle, my help's sister, is already there."

"Mrs Tickle – is that really her name?" asked Snubby. "Is she ticklish?"

"I have no idea," said Mrs Martin. "And if I were you I wouldn't try to find out."

"I thought a cousin of Barney's was coming too," said Roger. "Where is he? Are we going to pick him up somewhere?"

"No. He has started a cold," said Mrs Martin. "He may be along in a day or two, but not today. You'll have to settle in without him."

This pleased everyone very much. They badly wanted to have a long, friendly talk with old Barney, and a strange cousin would have embarrassed them.

They piled into the estate car, and waved goodbye to Barney's grandmother and little Jinny, the monkey. Then away they drove over the snowy roads towards the white-clad hills.

"Wake me up at Rat-a-Tat House," said Snubby, suddenly feeling sleepy after his enormous lunch. "What fun we're going to have there!"

You're right, Snubby – you just wait and see!

5

Rat-a-Tat House

The car had to go slowly along some of the roads because they were already slippery. It took about an hour to reach the little village of Boffame, which was two or three miles from Rat-a-Tat House.

"Now we shall soon be there," said Barney's father, who was at the wheel. "My word, we had some fun at Rat-a-Tat House when I was a boy, and played there with my brother and sisters and cousins. You'll have fun too, Barnabas, with your friends."

They went through the little village, and then up a small, very steep hill. The car stopped halfway up, and would not go on. Its wheels slid round and round in the same slippery place.

"Get the sacks out and the spade, children," said Mr Martin. "I thought this might happen, so we've come prepared!"

They got the spade and dug away the snow under the wheels, slipping the sacks beneath them instead. Then Mr Martin started up the car again, the wheels gripped the sacks instead of the slippery snow, and the car slowly reached the top of the hill. It stopped and Mr Martin waited for the children to come along to the car with the sacks and spade.

"It's a good thing I took all the food and things that you'll need to Rat-a-Tat House yesterday," he said. "I doubt if a car will be able to get through if we have any more snow."

"Perhaps we shall be cut off from everywhere!" said Snubby in delight. "Lost in the snowy hills. Marooned in Rat-a-Tat House. We shan't be able to go back to school. Hurrah!"

Loony barked joyfully. If anyone said "hurrah" it meant they were happy, so he had to join in too. Miranda leaned across the car and tweaked one of his long ears, and there was a scrimmage immediately. Mr Martin looked round for a moment. "I don't know what's happening at the back, but it's most disturbing to the driver," he remarked, and Loony at once got a smack from Snubby, and yelped in surprise.

The car went slowly on. They came to another hill – would the car stick halfway up this time? No, it went up steadily and everyone gave a sigh of relief.

The countryside looked enchanting in its thick blanket of dazzling white snow. Every little twig was outlined in white, and every sharp outline of fence or roof was softened by the snow. Diana looked out of the window and thought how beautiful it was.

"We'll have marvellous tobogganing," said Roger. "Best we've ever had. And plenty of skating if the frost holds."

"It's sure to," said Barney's father, driving the car down into a little valley surrounded by snow-clad hills on every side. "Now we're nearly there, you'll see Rat-a-Tat House in a minute, it's round this corner. Ah, there's the frozen lake, look."

"Oh, it's quite a big lake!" said Diana, surprised. "What a pity we can't go boating and swimming, as well as skating."

Everyone laughed. "Rather impossible," said Barney's father. "Perhaps you can come again in the summer and have some fun with Barney and his cousins then."

"So this is the house," said Snubby, in approval, as they swung in at a small drive. "Ha! I like it! It's – it's rather odd looking, isn't it? All those turrets and towers and tucked-in windows and things."

"It's old," said Mr Martin, "but was so very sturdily built that it has lasted well for a great many years. Oliver Cromwell once stayed here, and it is said that a celebrated Spaniard, who was taken prisoner, was brought here and hidden – and what is more, was never heard of again!"

"Gosh!" said Snubby, thrilled. "I hope he isn't still there. I can't speak a word of Spanish. I rather like the look of Rat-a-Tat House. I feel as if plenty of exciting things have happened here."

As they swung slowly up the drive, the front door opened and someone stood there smiling at them – a very small woman with a plait of dark hair wound round on top of her head, and merry dark eyes. She wore a flowered overall, and over it a spotless white apron. The children liked her at once.

"Is that Mrs Tickle?" asked Snubby, leaping out of the car before anyone else.

"Yes," said Barney. "But don't ask her if she's ticklish, because hundreds of people have asked that already and she's tired of it. Hello, Mrs Tickle! I hope you haven't been lonely."

"Not a bit of it, I've been too busy!" said the little woman, coming to help with the suitcases. "Are you cold? Come away in, then, I've a nice fire for you. Good afternoon, Mr Martin – I'm right glad to see you all, I was afraid you'd not get through the snow."

"We were only stuck once," said Mr Martin. "I'll just see the children in safely, Mrs Tickle, and then I must go, because I want to get away before more snow falls. It looks as if the sky is full of it again."

"That's right, sir, you get home before it's

dark," said little Mrs Tickle. "Oh, my word, who's this?"

It was Loony, prancing round in the snow, getting in everyone's way as usual.

"I didn't know you were bringing a dog," said Mrs Tickle. "I've got no dog biscuits for him."

"Oh, he doesn't mind having what we have," Snubby assured her. "He loves a slice off the joint or a chop."

Mrs Tickle looked quite horrified. "He won't be getting anything like that while I'm in charge!" she said, leading them all indoors. "I like dogs to be kept in their place. And monkeys too," she said, with a look at Miranda sitting on Barney's shoulder. "Well, here you are – sit down and warm yourselves!"

She led them into a big panelled room, at one end of which was an enormous fireplace with a fire of logs, crackling and blazing.

"Oh, it's lovely!" said Diana, glancing all round. "It's like a house in a storybook. And how light the room is!"

"That's the reflection from the snow outside," said Mrs Tickle.

Loony was growling in a most peculiar manner and backing away from the fireplace, towards which he had run for warmth. Barney gave a bellow of laughter.

"Look! He's just seen the bearskin rug in front of the fire! It's got the bear's head at

one end and he thinks it's real!"

Certainly poor Loony had had a terrible shock! He had run towards the fire, and had suddenly seen the old bearskin rug, and two glass eyes in the bear's head shining balefully at him. Loony imagined that the bear was crouching down ready to spring, and had backed away at once, producing his fiercest growls.

"Idiot," said Snubby. "Look at Miranda – she's braver than you are, Loony!"

Miranda had also seen the bear – but she had seen bearskin rugs before and was not at all worried. She leaped down and sat on the bear's head, chattering away at Loony, and jigging up and down.

"She's telling you not to be such a coward, Loony," said Snubby, severely. "Really, I'm ashamed of you!"

"Well, children, Mrs Tickle will take you all round the house and show you your rooms," said Barney's father, looking at his watch. "And no doubt she has a fine tea waiting. Help her all you can, please. Barney, you are in charge here, remember, and if anything goes wrong, let me know at once."

"Yes, Dad," said Barney.

"You'll be quite all right," said his father. "Mrs Tickle knows where the toboggans are, and your skates – we brought them here when we drove her over with all the food and bedclothes and so on. Well, have a good time. Mrs Tickle, keep them in order and don't stand any nonsense."

"I'll keep them in order all right, Mr Martin," said little Mrs Tickle, looking quite fierce. Then she smiled. "I'll enjoy having them round me," she said. "Mine are all grown up now, and it will be like old times to have them rampaging round. I hope you get back all right, sir."

They all went to see Mr Martin off in the car. It was getting dark already, though the gleaming snow threw its white light everywhere. "Goodbye!" shouted everyone, and waved till the car had crawled out of the gate.

They all went back into the fire-lit sitting-room, with its wide windowseats, its enormous fireplace, and gleaming old furniture. Snubby stood by the fire, rubbing his hands in glee.

"Isn't this brilliant?" he said. "I wish we could go out into the snow now and toboggan. Fancy sliding down those hills at top speed. Loony, do you think you'll like tobogganing?"

Loony had no idea what tobogganing was, but he was sure he would like anything that Snubby liked. He felt the general excitement and decided to show off. He rushed round the room at top speed, barking, and suddenly lost his footing on the highly polished floor, rolled over and finished by sliding along swiftly on his back. Everyone roared.

"Is that how you're going to slide over the snow?" said Snubby. "You'll get along fine like that, Loony."

"Would you like to come and unpack?" said Mrs Tickle's voice at the door. "And by that time, you'll be ready for tea, I've no doubt!"

She was right – they certainly would!

6

Settling In

A wide staircase led up to the first floor of Rat-a-Tat House, and many rooms opened off the upstairs landing. Everywhere there was panelling, and Snubby went along knocking at the walls, *rat-a-tat-tat*!

"Snubby, must you do that?" said Diana. "What's the idea?"

"Secret passages of course!" said Snubby at once. "You never know! This place might be riddled with them!"

"Well, I hope you're not going to knock on the walls every time you pass them," said Diana.

"It's Rat-a-Tat House, isn't it?" said Snubby, with a grin, and knocked again on some wooden panelling – *rat-a-tat-tat*! "I say, I wonder why it's got such a peculiar name? Do you know, Barney?"

"No," said Barney. "But maybe Mrs Tickle does. We'll ask her sometime."

Mrs Tickle was away along the landing opening doors as she went. "You can choose your own rooms!" she called. "Barney has one to himself, and so has Diana, but you other two boys are to share. The dog can sleep down in the kitchen."

"Well, he can't," muttered Snubby under his breath. "And what's more, he won't! He'll be sleeping on my bed as usual!"

The rooms were rather exciting. They all had panelled walls, which Snubby proceeded to knock on smartly with his knuckles, cushioned windowseats, old-fashioned wash-stands, and cupboards that opened out of the panelling.

"You can hardly tell they're cupboards!" said Diana, opening hers. "They look just like part of the oak walls. I never had a room like this before. I feel as if I've slipped a few hundred years back in history!"

"Our room's smashing too," announced Snubby. "Where's Mrs Tickle? Oh, she's gone. Good. I just wanted to say something she's not to hear. I am not going to let her shut Loony up in the kitchen tonight, so I shall think of some way to prevent it – and then he can come on my bed as usual. He'd be miserable if he had to sleep in the kitchen."

Diana opened her suitcase and unpacked and put her things away neatly, while the boys explored the other part of the house. Mrs Tickle called up the stairs: "Tea will be ready in five minutes, and the scones are hot, so don't be too long."

Diana shouted for the others. "Roger – Barney – Snubby! Tea's ready, so hurry up and unpack!"

Roger and Barney came along and put their things away in the great old chests and dark cupboards. Snubby rushed up with Loony at the very last minute, covered with dust and cobwebs.

"Where in the world have you been?" said Diana, looking at him in disgust. "Don't come near me, please! You're so cobwebby that you've probably got spiders crawling all over you!"

"Am I?" said Snubby, surprised, and brushed himself down so vigorously that dust flew everywhere. "I found a little attic place – rather exciting, with old boxes and trunks in it. Hey, what's that!"

It was the booming sound of the old gong in the hall. Mrs Tickle was tired of waiting for them to come down and had suddenly remembered the gong. How it made them jump! Miranda leaped to the top of the curtains at once, and Loony ran under the bed.

"That's calling us for tea, I expect," said Diana. "Snubby, you've got to unpack your suitcase and put your things away before you come down. Go on, now – hurry up!"

"All right, all right, teacher," said Snubby. "Don't start trying to boss me! It won't take me long to unpack."

It didn't. He simply undid his suitcase, opened his cupboard door, and emptied everything into it. He shoved the suitcase in at the back and then shot downstairs at top speed, Loony just in front of him. The staircase ended in a wide, polished hall, and Loony was able to slide all the way to the front with the greatest ease.

"Jolly good, Loony," said Snubby, admiringly, and walked sedately into the sitting-room, where the others were just about to sit down. Diana stared at him accusingly.

"You haven't had time to unpack. You go back and do it!"

"Everything is safely in my cupboard," said Snubby. "And the suitcase is empty, teacher!"

"Don't keep calling me that," said Diana exasperated, but Snubby didn't even hear. His attention had been caught by the meal on the tea table. On a spotless white cloth were six different plates of food. Where Diana was sitting was a very large brown teapot, a large blue milk jug, and a large basin of sugar lumps. Two dishes of jam were on the table and one pot of honey.

Snubby looked in awe at the six plates of food. "Stacks of new bread and butter, hot buttered scones – at least three each, gingerbread squares – all brown and sticky, a giant of a chocolate cake, a jam sponge twice as large as usual, and home-made macaroons! Macaroons – my very favourite goody. Hey, Mrs Tickle, Mrs Tickle!"

And the delighted Snubby with Loony at his heels went rushing into the kitchen to a surprised Mrs Tickle to tell her what he thought of the tea. He debated whether to give her a hug, but decided that he didn't know her well enough yet.

Mrs Tickle was very pleased with his admiration of the first meal she had provided. "Go along with you," she said, beaming. "You're a caution, you are! You'd better be careful that the others haven't eaten everything by the time you get back to the table!"

That made Snubby rush off in a panic, but to his relief there was still plenty left. He had to gobble to catch up with them, but Snubby never minded that.

"Your table manners haven't improved at all," said Diana primly. She felt quite like her mother, sitting in state behind the big brown teapot.

"Sorry, teacher," said Snubby, in such a humble voice that everyone laughed. "I'll stay in and write out 'I must please dear Diana, I must please dear Diana' one hundred times!"

"I shall throw something at you in a minute," said Diana. "Probably the teapot."

"Right," said Snubby. "But wait till it's empty. I may want another cup of tea. I say, look at Miranda, Barney, she's dipping her fingers into the strawberry jam and then licking them."

"Miranda, how can you?" said Barney, reprovingly, and the little monkey hid her face in his neck as if she was ashamed – but the next minute, down went her little paw into the jam-dish again!

It was a happy, merry tea, and Barney enjoyed it more than any of them. He had been a lonely boy for so many years, longing for the companionship, the teasing, the family talk that he had never had. Now he was quite at home in the fun, and entered into the teasing with delight. But nobody ever had a readier answer than the cheeky, irrepressible Snubby – he was never at a loss as to what to say or do!

They all helped Mrs Tickle to clear away tea, then went back into the sitting-room. "If you want more wood for the fire, it's in that cupboard there, by the fireplace. I'll bring you more from outside if you want it," said Mrs Tickle.

"No, you won't," said Roger at once. "I'll do that – and just tell us whatever jobs you want done, Mrs Tickle, and we'll do them straight away."

"That's what I like to hear!" said the little woman, pleased, and went out smiling.

Soon they were all sitting round the fire. "Let's have a game," said Snubby. "I

brought some cards. I'll go and fetch them."
He went off upstairs, knocking on the panelling all the way – *knock-knock-knock* –
rat-a-tat-tat, rat-a-tat-tat!

"I wish he wouldn't," said Diana. "Why
does Snubby always have to make some
kind of noise?"

Snubby came back with the cards, and
the children heard his *knock-knock-knock*
on the panelling again.

Loony listened with his head on one side
and so did Miranda. It was rather an eerie
sound, hollow and irritating.

"Let's put some more wood on the fire
before we begin," said Roger, and opened
the door of the little cupboard beside the
fireplace, where the logs were kept. He
hauled one out, threw it on the fire and
shut the cupboard door. Then he went with
the others to the table and they all sat down
to play cards.

But they hadn't dealt more than one hand
when something made them jump. It was a
hollow, knocking sound: *knock-knock-knock*
– *rat-a-tat-tat! Knock-knock-knock* – *rat-a-
tat-tat!*

Loony growled, and that made them all
jump, too. It wasn't Snubby knocking this
time – he was there at the table with them,
listening, half scared.

"It must be Mrs Tickle knocking or hammering something in the kitchen!" said

Roger, realising that Diana was frightened.

"It isn't," said his sister in a low voice. "It's in this room. But there's nobody here but us!"

Knock-knock-knock – rat-a-tat-tat! It was exactly the same knocking as Snubby had drummed on the panelling when he went up and down the stairs.

"It *is* in this room," said Barney, starting up. "Whatever can it be? Who is it? I don't like it."

"Let's get Mrs Tickle," said Roger, and shouted for her. "Mrs Tickle! We need you. Quickly!"

In came Mrs Tickle, most surprised. "Whatever is the matter?" she said, seeing their startled faces.

"Listen," said Roger, as the soft *knock-knock-knock* came again. "That knocking, Mrs Tickle . . . what can it be?"

7

Knock-Knock-Knock!

Mrs Tickle stood in the middle of the room, listening. She looked alarmed. "The knocking!" she said. "The knocking! It's come again after all these years!"

"Whatever do you mean, Mrs Tickle?" said Barney. "My father didn't tell me about any knocking and he knows all about this house."

"Maybe he doesn't know about the knocking, though," said Mrs Tickle, looking relieved as the noise stopped. "I heard the tale in the village of Boffame yesterday. It's because of the knocking that this house got its name."

"Sit down, Mrs Tickle, and tell us," said Barney, and the little woman sat down at once, on the very edge of a chair. She began to speak again in a low voice.

"I'm only telling you what's said," she said. "A tale that's handed down through the years, you understand. I heard it from old John Hurdie, in the post office, and he got it from his great-granny, so he said."

"Go on, go on," said Roger, as she stopped for breath. A piece of wood broke in the flames of the fire and the burning log fell to the bottom of the hearth, making them all jump.

"Well," said Mrs Tickle, "it's said that the house was called Boffame House after the lake and the village – but soon after people came to live here, there were strange knock-ings on the front door—"

"On the front door?" said Roger. "Do you mean someone hammered on it with their fists?"

"No. They used the great knocker there," said Mrs Tickle. "Didn't you see it when you came in this afternoon?"

"The door was wide open, so we didn't notice," said Diana, trying to remember. "Is it a very big knocker?"

"Enormous," said Mrs Tickle. "And you wouldn't believe the sound it makes – thun-derous, Mr Hurdie at the post office told me. But when the footman went to answer the door all those years ago and see who was there – there was nobody."

"The one who knocked might have run away," said Snubby, hopefully. "Lots of people do knock at doors or ring bells, and then run away. They think it's funny."

"Well, it isn't, it's stupid," said Mrs Tickle. "We've got a boy in our village who does that but he did it once too often to me. Aha – I put glue all round the knocker! What a mess he was in!"

Everyone laughed. "But why didn't the person who knocked all those years ago stay till the door was opened?" asked Snubby. "And who was he?"

"Nobody ever saw him, though often he came knocking day or night," said Mrs Tickle, enjoying the telling of such a dramatic story. "And what was more, that knocking went on for a hundred and fifty years, so the old story goes!"

"Ha – then it couldn't have been the same person knocking all that time," said Snubby. "But what did the knocking mean – anything at all?"

"Yes, it was said to give warning that there was a traitor in the house!" said Mrs Tickle. "So there must have been a good many traitors then, it seems to me! And old Mr Hurdie, he says that when the knocking came, there was always a searching of the old place to see if anyone was hiding there, and the servants were always questioned to find out if one of them was untrustworthy. Oh, there were some goings-on in those old days, you mark my words."

"How long ago did the knocking stop?" asked Barney. "You said it only lasted a hundred and fifty years but this house is much older than that."

"It's well over a hundred years ago now since Mr No One hammered at the door with that knocker!" said Mrs Tickle. "It's so old now that I reckon it would fall off the door if anyone touched it!"

Mrs Tickle's story was so very interesting that the children had quite forgotten about the mysterious knocking they themselves had heard a little while back – but they soon remembered it when it suddenly came again!

Knock-knock-knock – rat-a-tat-tat! There it was again, soft and hollow and mysterious – and somewhere in the room! There wasn't a doubt of it.

Barney sprang up at once. "We've got to find what it is!" he said.

"Oh dear!" said Mrs Tickle, beginning to tremble at the knees. "Oh dear, I've gone and scared myself with that old story. I'm all of a shake. It's the knocker back again – Mr No One after all these years. But what's he knocking for? There's no traitor here!"

"Cheer up!" said Roger. "He's not knocking at the front door, Mrs Tickle. Come on, Barney – let's trace where the knocking is!"

They waited for it to come again and it did, as soon as they were quite silent. *Knock-knock-knock – rat-a-tat-tat!*

"It's over there – in that corner of the room!" said Barney, and ran towards the corner. The knocking stopped and then began again. *Knock-knock-knock.*

"It's coming from the wood cupboard!" cried Mrs Tickle. "Bless us all, that's where it's coming from. But there's only logs there, that I do know."

"We'll soon see," said Barney grimly, and flung open the little door of the wood cupboard.

And out sprang a very indignant and rather frightened Miranda! The little monkey ran chattering to Barney and leaped straight to his shoulder, burying her little furry head in his neck.

"Miranda! *Miranda!* Why – it was only you in the cupboard after all," said Barney. "You little pest, you gave us such a fright! But why did you knock like that?"

"She was imitating Snubby!" cried Diana. "She heard him keep on knocking on the panelling as he went up and downstairs – you know how she loves to copy what we do – so when she got shut in that cupboard, she did what Snubby did and knocked on the wooden door in exactly the same way – *knock-knock-knock – rat-a-tat-tat*!"

"That's it," said Roger, most relieved. "Phew – I didn't like it much. When did Miranda get shut in?"

"When you opened the wood cupboard door to put more logs on the fire," said Barney. "She must have slipped in without your noticing it, and you shut the door on her. Funny little thing – knocking like that!"

"Well, I hope she doesn't do anything else to give us such a scare," said Mrs Tickle, looking herself again. "Right feared I was! And don't you start thinking about that big old knocker on the front door – Mr No One hasn't been at it for a hundred years, and it's not likely he'll start now."

"Anyway, there are no traitors in this house now," said Barney. "Only four kids, you, Mrs Tickle, and a monkey and a dog. Miranda, don't do such an idiotic thing again. I'm surprised we didn't miss you, but

I quite thought you were asleep in that rug on the sofa."

"Why didn't Loony go to the cupboard and scratch at it as he usually does when he hears a noise coming from somewhere?" wondered Diana.

"Easy," said Snubby, with a grin. "He's not awfully keen on getting Miranda out of trouble! I bet he thought she could jolly well stay there as long as possible!"

"Yes, I believe you're right," said Barney, looking at Loony, who was busy scratching himself. "Bad dog, Loony – to let poor little Miranda stay in the dark cupboard without lifting a paw to help her."

"Wuff," said Loony politely, and went on scratching. Snubby poked him with his foot.

"Stop it!" he said. "Sit up and listen when you're spoken to."

Loony wagged his tail, and it thumped on the floor – *knock-knock-knock*!

"Oh my goodness – don't you start rat-tat-tat-ting now!" said Snubby, and Diana giggled. She was very relieved to find that their scare had been groundless – and she half wished that Mrs Tickle hadn't told them that strange old story.

"Let's get on with our game," said Snubby. "Let me see – we'd better deal again. Come on!"

They dealt again, and Snubby looked at his cards. "Ha!" he exclaimed. "Couldn't be better! I can tell you this – even if Mr No One comes and hammers on that knocker now, I shall go on with this game – I've got a great hand!"

Fortunately for him, there was no hammering at the front door, and he won the game easily, looking very pleased with himself.

It was cosy and warm in the sitting-room, with the log fire blazing away. The children felt very happy, thinking of the next day and all the fun they would have. Diana drew the curtains after a while, shutting out the starry night and the white snow.

Later on Mrs Tickle came in with a tray. "Supper!" she said, beaming. "Will you lay the table for me, Diana, while I go and see to the poached eggs?"

"Poached eggs! Mrs Tickle, how did you know I was simply longing for one?" said Snubby at once.

"Well, I had a feeling you were longing for two, not one," said Mrs Tickle, who had taken quite a liking to the snub-nosed, freckle-faced "imp" as she called him to herself. Snubby grinned in delight.

"Two! How well you know me already!" he said. "Loony – salute Mrs Tickle, please – your very best salute!"

And Loony, proud to show off his very newest trick, sat up and saluted quite smartly, much to Miranda's interest.

"There now – he's as sharp as his master!" said Mrs Tickle, putting down her tray and laughing. "You're cautions, both of you. I'll be back with the poached eggs in a minute." And off she went, chuckling over Snubby and Loony. Really – what a pair!

8

What Fun!

Supper was a very pleasant meal, a simple one of poached eggs, hot chocolate, and biscuits and butter. Diana began to yawn before she was halfway through it. Miranda immediately copied her, yawning delicately, showing her tiny white teeth, and patting her mouth as she did so, just like Diana.

Both Miranda and Loony were enjoying a buttered biscuit. Each of them licked the butter off first, Loony with his large pink tongue and Miranda very daintily with her tiny, curling one.

"Not very good manners," said Roger lazily. "My word, I'm sleepy. It's this big fire, I suppose. Snubby, how are you going to prevent Loony having to sleep down in the kitchen? I bet Mrs Tickle will insist on it."

She did, of course. She appeared at ten o'clock. "Time for you all to go up," she announced firmly. "And I'll take that dog to the kitchen now, Snubby."

"You won't mind if he chews up the rug there, and the cushion on the chair and any slippers or towels you've left out, will you, Mrs Tickle?" said Snubby solemnly. "I'll pay for them all, of course, if he does much damage – but it's very, very hard on my pocket."

Mrs Tickle was taken aback. She looked down at Loony, who stared back at her unwinkingly.

"He can't help being a nibbly, chewy dog," said Snubby earnestly. "It's his nature, you see. The funny thing is, he never chews anything when he sleeps with me. Never."

Mrs Tickle made up her mind at once. "Well, you let him sleep with you then," she said, "if you can abide a smelly dog in your bedroom. I won't have him chewing up my kitchen, and that's flat."

"I'll do anything to please you," said Snubby, rather overdoing it now. "Anything. I'll even have a smelly dog in my bedroom. Won't I, Loony?"

Loony thumped his tail on the floor and Miranda at once pounced on it. Loony swung round at her and she leaped on his back, hanging on to his silky fur for all she was worth.

Loony raced round the room with her on his back, trying hard to remember how to unseat her. "Roll on the floor, ass!" cried Snubby. "Roll on the floor!"

But, as soon as Loony rolled over, Miranda was off like a bird, springing here and there until she came back to Barney's shoulder.

"Good as a play they are!" said Mrs Tickle, laughing. "Now – are you coming up or not?"

"Right," said Barney, getting up. "Come on, everyone."

He waited till they were all in the hall, then put out the lights in the sitting-room. Miranda was annoying everyone by switching the hall light on and off and leaving them in darkness.

"Hey, Barney!" called Snubby indignantly. "Come and stop this fat-headed monkey from playing with the light. She must be dotty!"

Miranda was safely captured, and then the little procession made its way up the wide staircase. Loony tearing on ahead as usual, and Miranda firmly tucked in Barney's right arm.

"Goodnight!" he said. "Sleep well. We're all near one another, so if anyone's scared in the night, give a yell!"

But they were all far too sleepy to be scared by anything. The beds were very comfortable, and there were plenty of blankets to keep out the cold, for the rooms were none too warm. Snubby decided that he would tidy his belongings in the morning; it would take him so long now to sort them out from the heap he had thrown on the floor of his cupboard!

Loony was already asleep on the middle of the bed. Snubby pushed him firmly down to the end and then got into bed himself, quite pleased at the warm patch Loony had made in the middle. He lay for half a minute, wondering at the utter quiet and stillness of the old house – not a sound to be heard, not one!

How awful if the great old knocker began to knock as in the olden days! Snubby was giving himself quite a pleasant thrill about this when he suddenly fell sound asleep – so sound that he didn't even feel Loony creeping up the bed and lying heavily on his middle.

The morning was bright and clear and the sun shone so brilliantly that the snow on the pond began to melt fast. "That's good," said Roger, looking out of his window as he dressed. "If the snow melts on the pond and we get no more, it will freeze again tonight and we can skate tomorrow, because the ice will be free of snow. Today we'll go tobogganing."

After an excellent breakfast of porridge, bacon, eggs and toast, they went to see what jobs they could do for Mrs Tickle. Her kitchen was enormous, and still had a pump at one end for the old sink. At the other was a large old kitchen range, but beside it was a modern cooker on which she cooked everything.

She had the fire going in the range to heat the kitchen, and it all looked very cheerful. She looked up as the children came in carrying the breakfast things and smiled all over her pleasant face.

"What else can we do for you?" asked Diana. "I'll help you with the washing-up."

"Well, you don't need to do that," said Mrs Tickle. "But if you could see that you each make your bed – and get some wood in for me – that would be fine. I'll be able to get on well then."

"Upstairs everyone," ordered Diana, taking charge. "Roger, you get Snubby to help you with your bed, then you help him with his – or he'll just leave it as it is. Do you hear, Snubby?"

"No, teacher," said Snubby, and skipped out of the way of a slap from Diana.

Everything was soon done, and well done too. Snubby's bed was as well made as the others and so much wood was brought in that Mrs Tickle said she had almost enough for a week! She was very pleased. Snubby decided that he now knew her well enough to give her a hug.

"Now then, get away with you," she said, surprised. "Squeezing all the breath out of me like that. You're a caution, that's what you are. Oh, bless us all, there's that dog got my brush again. I'll give him such a lar-ruping if I catch him."

But she never could catch the artful Loony. He enjoyed himself running off with her brush, her duster, and her mop – till she took to keeping a big broom at hand and chasing him every time he appeared.

"Let's go and get our things on now," said Roger, when all the jobs were done. "I'm longing to get out into the snow. Let's toboggan first of all, before we have a snowball fight or anything."

It wasn't long before they were all in their outdoor things – wellington boots, scarves, gloves, thick jerseys. It was bitterly cold out of the sun, but they soon got warm.

They had two toboggans – each big enough to take two or three of them at once. They set off up the nearest hill, drag-ging the toboggans behind them. Loony tried to gallop off at a furious speed as usual, but to his dismay found that his legs sank right into this soft white stuff that so mysteriously covered the ground – and for once he had to move very slowly indeed.

Miranda wouldn't leave Barney's shoulder. She didn't like the snow, though it did occur to her that it would be fun to put some down Barney's neck. She kept her little paws under his collar to warm them. Barney liked feeling them there.

The hill was steep enough to give the

children a very exciting run down to the bottom. There they all tumbled off into the snow, roaring with laughter. Loony soon learned to sit on the toboggan with Roger and Snubby, his long ears flying backwards in the wind. He loved it, and barked all the way down.

Miranda went with Barney and Diana. She was a bit scared of the sudden rush down the hill and cuddled under Barney's coat, her tiny head just peeping out. "You're scared, Miranda!" said Barney. But when he tried to make her stay behind at the top of the hill, she wouldn't. No, she wanted to be with Barney every minute of the time.

They had races on their toboggans – two on each toboggan, and then one on each. Barney won easily. His brilliant blue eyes were bluer than ever on this dazzling snowy day, and he looked very happy. In fact, they were all very happy. It was Snubby, as usual, who was the first to feel the pangs of hunger.

"You can't be hungry already," said Roger. "Not after that colossal breakfast, Snubby. Why, you had six pieces of toast on top of everything else. It can't possibly be lunch-time yet." He undid his glove to look at his watch.

But at that moment a bell sounded clearly through the frosted air: Mrs Tickle ringing to tell them lunch was ready.

"What did I tell you?" said Snubby, triumphantly. "I don't need to look at the time to know when a meal's due. Come on, Loony – race you to Rat-a-Tat House!"

9

A Happy Day

"What a lovely smell," said Snubby as soon as he reached Rat-a-Tat House. "What is it?"

"Stew!" said Roger, sniffing. And stew it was, full of carrots and onions and turnips and parsnips. Loony almost pulled everything off the table in his anxiety to see what it was that smelled so good.

"Now you stop that!" ordered Mrs Tickle, pushing him away just in time. "If you come out to the kitchen with me you'll see I've got some delicious stew-bones for you. Paws off the tablecloth, please."

"I'm quite tired," said Diana, sitting down with a flop. "Aren't you, Barney?"

"No, not really," said Barney. "But I'm used to a strenuous sort of life and you're not. I remember the days when I was a hoop-la boy and got up at half past five to help to get the fair ready – worked all the morning – took charge of the hoop-la stall in the afternoon, and after that worked as gate-boy, taking the money – and then helped the fellow on the swing-boats."

"Oh, Barney – your life must seem so different now," said Diana, beginning to eat her stew. "Barney, didn't you feel odd when your father first found you and took you home to a family you didn't know?"

"Yes, I did," said Barney. "I was shy for the first time in my life, I reckon. I couldn't seem to shake hands properly, or say how-do-you-do, or even look them in the face – except my grandmother. I wasn't shy of her. But I guess that was partly because she had a monkey on her shoulder like me – and the two monkeys took to one another from the first. They even shook paws."

"Are your cousins nice?" asked Snubby, holding out his plate for a second helping of stew.

"Yes. Very," said Barney. "You know – it was strange I've never been ashamed of being a circus-boy, or of any of the jobs I've ever done in my life, but when I met my clean and tidy cousins – they even had clean nails – and saw their nice manners, well, I sort of felt ashamed, and wished I could sink into the ground."

"You didn't!" said Snubby, surprised. "I bet you're worth six of any of your cousins. Why, you're even worth six of me and Roger. I think you're a marvel."

"You may be a bit of an ass, Snubby, but

you're a real sport," said Barney, touched. "But I'll tell you a peculiar thing – instead of my cousins looking down on me because I'd lived in caravans and tents, and done all kinds of odd circus jobs, they thought it was all marvellous, and they were proud of having me for their cousin. Think of that!"

"You deserve it," said Diana. "You had a jolly hard time, and you were all alone but you never gave up. I *am* glad we met you that day – it seems so long ago now. We've had some exciting times together, haven't we, Barney?"

"Yes," said Barney, getting up to take some things to the kitchen. "But I'm afraid they're ended now. When things run smoothly and happily there don't seem to be many adventures – or mysteries."

Snubby forgot his manners and pointed his fork at him. "How do you know? Saying things like that is enough to make things begin to happen at once. I smell something in the air."

"Yes, you smell the remains of the stew," said Barney, laughing. "Get up, you lazy fellow, and help me to take these things out and get the pudding."

"Right," said Snubby and stood up. "Gosh!" he said in surprise. "Something's happened to my legs – I can hardly stand on them."

Roger and Diana found exactly the same

thing. Their legs were stiff, and hurt when they walked. Barney laughed at them.

"It's all that trudging up the snowy hills," he said. "We must have walked up and tobogganed down fifty or sixty times. You'll be as stiff as anything for a day or two."

"I can't possibly walk up even the smallest hill this afternoon," groaned Snubby, in dismay. "Honestly, I think I'll have to have crutches."

"I can't go tobogganing any more today, that's certain," said Diana, sinking into a chair. "But, oh – I don't want to miss being out of doors on such a heavenly day."

"Cheer up," said Barney. "We'll go out and build an enormous snowman and we'll have a snowball fight – you'll find you can do that all right!"

Barney was right. Although they found they could hardly walk when they left the table to stagger out with the dirty plates to Mrs Tickle, their legs gradually became less stiff and by the time they went out into the snow again they could walk quite well – though none of them except Barney felt that they could possibly climb up a hill dragging a toboggan behind them.

"The snow's just right for snowballing!" called Diana, gathering some into her gloved hand. They all wore waterproof gloves, knowing from experience how woollen ones became soaked at once, and then the cold bit their fingers and chilled them through and through.

"I'll take Diana for my side, and you two can be together," said Barney. "Diana, you can make me snowball ammunition, and I'll do the throwing. Look, this is our little fort. If we are driven out of it the other side have won – but we'll stand firm!"

He made a big circle for himself and Diana, and Roger and Snubby made one for themselves too. Miranda was on Barney's side, of course, and Loony was on the other side.

Ammunition was soon made and the battle began. Snubby was a very wild thrower, but Roger was excellent, and most of his snowballs found their mark. Diana gasped and ducked and yelled, while Barney tried to protect her by sending a fast volley at Roger. Miranda was puzzled by the fight, and finding herself in a dangerous place on Barney's shoulder, leaped off to a nearby tree.

She landed on a snowy branch, and watched the fight with great interest, sometimes jigging up and down on the branch and scattering snow from the tree.

Loony, of course, went completely mad as he always did when there was any kind of contest between the children. He floundered about, getting in everyone's way, and finally, for some reason of his own, dug an

enormous hole in the snow, sending it flying out behind him as if he were a rabbit digging a burrow.

The fight went on until Barney became too strong for Roger, and leaving his own circle, advanced on the two panting boys, sending a stream of well-directed snowballs at them.

"Pax, pax!" yelled Snubby, as Diana also advanced, and snowballed him mercilessly as he slipped and rolled in the snow.

"All right – you win!" panted Roger, collapsing into the snow. "Gosh, that was the best snowball fight I've ever had! Pax, Diana, pax – don't you dare put that down my neck. Help, Loony, help!"

The funniest thing that happened that afternoon was when Miranda suddenly discovered the meaning of all this snowballing. She had sat on her tree, watching the others in astonishment as they rolled the snow into balls, and hurled them through the air – and all at once she understood the game.

Quickly she leaped off the bough and gathered up some snow in her tiny paws, making a tight little snowball – and then, with a very good aim, she flung it straight at Loony, and hit him, *biff*, on the nose. He gasped and spluttered in surprise.

"Good shot, Miranda!" yelled Barney, and laughed his infectious laugh. "Did you see that, you others? Miranda threw a snowball at Loony and hit him. Look out, Loony, she's made another."

Miranda thought this was a wonderful way of teasing Loony but soon her fingers began to feel very cold indeed, and whimpering with the pain in them, she leaped up to Barney's shoulders, and stuffed her cold paws down his warm neck.

"Hey!" he said, startled. "Are you putting snow down my neck, Miranda? You'd better not. Oh, they're your cold, cold paws – all right, warm them, then!"

The snow was exactly right for building a snowman too. Snubby had the ambitious idea of building a snow house as well, alongside the snowman.

"You build the snowman, Barney; you and Miranda and Diana," said Snubby. "Roger and I will build his house – a proper little snow house with a chimney and everything."

Barney and Diana set to work on the snowman, and made a fat fellow, with a large round head and big feet sticking out at the bottom. "His name is Mr Icy-Cold," said Diana, with a giggle. "Let's get him a hat."

Roger and Snubby were hard at work on their snow house. They had borrowed two shovels from Mrs Tickle, which made the building a good deal quicker.

Soon they had built the rounded walls, as

high as themselves, and somehow managed to make a roof that stayed on – a rounded one, like an igloo. They also added a little chimney.

"Now a window," said Snubby, excited. "Get away, Loony. Go and mess about with the snowman, not with us. You'll find yourself being built into the roof soon!"

They made a little round window, and left a round opening for an entrance. They were really quite proud of their work when they had finished.

"It's a proper snow house," said Snubby, pleased. "Big enough to sit in. Come on, Roger, let's squeeze into it for a few minutes and see what it's like to live in a snow house."

They got inside, and sat down. Snubby peered out of the little window. "I can see our sitting-room window," he said. "And Mrs Tickle is inside, cleaning. Ooooh, I feel jolly cold! What about lighting a fire in our little house?"

That made Roger laugh. Loony came up to see what the joke was, and tried to squeeze himself in through the door and join them. He almost knocked down part of one wall and Snubby protested.

"You're so rough, Loony," he complained, pushing him out. "You ruined the snowman's feet by scrabbling for rabbits or something underneath them. I'll snowball you hard if you don't behave yourself."

"Come on," said Roger, "I'm getting cold sitting here. I can't imagine how people can live and sleep in an igloo – I should freeze to death."

He squeezed out carefully, followed by Snubby. Miranda came and watched them with interest. Now what were they doing? She hopped in through the window and then stared out cheekily. Loony made a rush at her, but Snubby caught his collar.

"No! If you and Miranda have a scrimmage in the snow house that will be the end of it. Roger, Barney, what about going in now? It must be nearly tea-time – or so the clock in my tummy tells me, and I could do with some scalding hot tea to drink."

It was a very tired set of children who sat down to a late tea – or an early supper – tired but happy. Diana said she could hardly lift the big brown teapot.

"We've forgotten to draw the curtains across the window," groaned Roger. "I meant to, and now I really feel I can't get out of my chair!"

The light from the big lamp over the table streamed out the window across the snow outside and just caught the outline of the snow house, and fell on the big snowman too.

"He looks as if he's watching us longingly," said Snubby. "I bet he'd like to come in and join us. Poor old Mr Icy-Cold!"

Snubby was just lifting his cup to his mouth, gazing out of the window as he did so, when he suddenly put down his cup again, and stared fixedly.

"Hey!" he said, startled. "Who's that out there – look, beyond my snow house? Somebody standing quite still. Look!"

Everyone looked, but no one could see anything or anyone. "It's only the snowman, ass," said Barney. "Don't scare Diana. Who on earth would come and stare at our window at this time of night in this lonely district?"

"I don't know," said Snubby, still gazing out. "I can't see anyone now. I suppose I must have been mistaken. But honestly, I thought there was someone standing quite still, watching us."

Barney got up and drew the curtains so that they met. "I tell you, it's only our snowman," he said. "Anyway, it can't be very nice for the poor thing to stand out in the cold and watch us eating a grand meal like this in the warm room. Goodnight, Mr Icy-Cold. See you in the morning."

10

Whose Glove?

"It can't have been anyone," said Diana. "Loony would have barked."

"Yes. So he would," said Snubby, relieved. "It was just my imagination."

Both Barney and Roger forebore to say that Loony would probably not hear any footsteps in the snow, and certainly could not see anyone out of the window. They didn't want to scare Diana, and they both honestly thought that Snubby had made a mistake.

All the same, Barney resolved to go and have a look-round for footprints in the morning – if it was possible to make out any strange ones amid the marks made by their own feet. The talk soon went on to something else, and they all forgot about Snubby's fright. They enjoyed their supper immensely and, as usual, carried out the dirty things to Mrs Tickle. Miranda collected the forks and handed them over proudly in her little paw.

"There now!" said Mrs Tickle delighted. "What a clever creature she is – but how you can wear her on your shoulder like that, Barney, I don't know, and her putting her hands down your neck too, to warm them!"

At half past nine everyone was asleep – but not in bed. No, they were all asleep in their chairs by the fire, books on their knees or fallen to the rug below. Loony too, was asleep, making little excited grunts as he chased a rat in his dreams. Miranda had cuddled under Barney's jumper and could not be seen, but she, too, was asleep.

There Mrs Tickle found them when she went in to ask if anyone wanted hot chocolate before they went to bed, for the night was really very cold.

"Do any of you want . . ." she began, and then chuckled to herself. Well, well, well – all fast asleep! They ought to be in their beds, poor things, tired out like that!

She woke them all, and to their great astonishment they found that they were not comfortably in bed as they imagined, but slumped in their chairs by the fire. So that was what a morning of tobogganing could do! Groaning and yawning, they went upstairs and crawled up to bed, with Mrs Tickle laughing at them and leading the way. What a set of yawners!

They all slept late the next morning, and

Mrs Tickle rang the gong in vain. In the end she had to go up and wake them all, and even pull Snubby out of bed and take all the clothes away!

However, they were all bright and cheery after breakfast, though all but Barney were very stiff. They gazed out of the window at the lake as they ate fried sausages and fried bread. The surface was quite free from snow and the ice looked blue and inviting.

"What about skating this morning?" said Barney. "Or are you all too stiff?"

"Well, I don't feel like using my aching muscles to climb up those hills in order to toboggan down them," said Diana. "But I'd like to try skating. I'll probably use a different set of muscles, and they won't hurt."

They did their usual jobs, and helped Mrs Tickle willingly. When she heard they were going skating she gave them each a packet of biscuits.

"Skating's hungry work," she said. "You'll need a snack – and maybe if you have that you won't want to eat me out of house and home when you get in for your lunch."

"I've got to stay behind and mend my sweater," said Diana. "I caught it yesterday and if I don't mend it before I go out it will all unravel. I'll catch you boys up later, down at the pond."

The others left her to ask Mrs Tickle for a needle, and went off with their skates. On the way they passed the big snowman they had built the day before, and stopped to look at him.

"He's a real beauty," said Barney. "Quite the biggest I've seen. We ought to have given him a coat to wear to make him look real."

"I say, just let's have a look and see if there *are* any strange footmarks about," said Roger, remembering Snubby's scare the night before.

"Oh no!" said Snubby, quite ashamed now of the alarm he had raised. "It was just that my eyes were tired with the glare of the snow, I expect. I saw things that weren't there!"

"We'll have a squint round, all the same," said Barney. He walked round the snowman, but saw nothing unusual at all – merely a large number of jumbled footmarks made by their wellington boots the day before.

Then he looked at the snow house and round about. There was again a mass of footsteps and it was impossible to tell whether any of them belonged to a stranger – though Barney's sharp eyes showed him one or two that he thought were not made by rubber boots. But no; it really was impossible to tell.

"Come on," he said. "Nothing here. Snubby must have been mistaken after all."

Snubby went into his little snow house

just for the fun of it. He sat down for a few moments, imagining that he was in an igloo. Then, hearing the others' voices getting faint in the distance, he stooped to go out through the doorway again.

And then it was that he saw the glove. There it lay, half hidden by the snow, just at the side of the little snow house. Snubby stared at it and picked it up, thinking for a moment that it must belong to Barney or Roger.

But it was a big glove – made of thick navy-blue wool. Not one of the children had hands large enough to fit the glove. Snubby turned it over, his heart beginning to beat fast. So there might have been someone out here last night after all – someone staring in through the lighted window, watching them. It wasn't at all a nice thought. He ran after the other two boys, shouting.

"Barney! Roger! Wait, I've got something to tell you!"

They turned round, recognising something urgent in his voice. Loony, who had run on with them, turned back at once and floundered over the snow to Snubby.

"What is it?" said Roger.

"Look what I found in my snow house," said Snubby, panting. "This glove! I was just crawling out when I found it. Surely it isn't one of ours – it's so big."

"No. It's not ours," said Roger. "We've

all got waterproof gloves, Barney too. This
is someone else's. I suppose Loony couldn't
possible have taken it from somewhere and
dropped it there, could he?"

"No. Not possibly," said Snubby. "He
didn't even go to the snow house with me.
He ran on with you. I say, you know – I
think there was someone out here last night
after all. But why? Out in all this cold and
snow."

"Don't say a word to Diana or Mrs
Tickle," said Roger. "You'll scare them stiff
if you do. This may be just nothing.
Anyway, we can't do anything about it now
– we'll just have to keep watch this evening
and see if we can spot anything. I must say
it's rather strange."

"Could somebody have crouched in the

snow house last night and watched us?" said Snubby. "I must have seen someone either getting in or getting out – I don't know which."

They sat down at the edge of the shining pond to put on their skates. Barney had some fine new ones given to him for Christmas by his grandmother. He had never skated in his life, and he was much looking forward to it. He puzzled over the glove that Snubby had found, but soon forgot about it as he stood up, wobbling, on his skates.

Snubby and Roger had skated before. Snubby, oddly enough, was better than Roger, and he was soon off and away, calling to the others.

Loony was most excited to see his master apparently flying over the ice, he went so fast and so lightly. With an excited bark he rushed over the snow to the ice and tried to bound after him. But to his surprise he found that all his four legs slid away beneath him, and there he was, sliding on his back, just as he did sometimes in a slippery hall.

However, it was much more difficult to find his feet again on the slippery pond than in a polished hall – each time he tried to stand he slipped over again, and at last he managed to sit down on his tail, looking very miserable.

"Bad luck, Loony!" shouted Snubby, circling round him. "You can't manage your legs this morning, can you? You'll have to learn to walk slowly for once."

But Loony leaped to his feet to follow Snubby, and again he found himself off balance, his paws slithering away beneath him, and his nose bumping the ground. He somehow managed to sit down again and howled dismally.

"All right, I'll take you back to the bank," said Snubby. "And just be sensible and stay there."

Roger was now on the ice, skating carefully, afraid of falling, but soon getting into the way of it. Barney stood and watched Snubby and the ease with which he flew over the ice. It looked to be just a question of balance and Barney knew all about that. Hadn't he walked the tightrope a thousand times? Hadn't he stood on horses' backs when they galloped gracefully around a circus ring?

Without another thought Barney stepped on to the ice and set off smoothly and rhythmically. Immediately he felt at home, and his feet felt as if they had wings. He gave a shout.

"Ho! This is wonderful! Why didn't I ever skate before?"

Roger and Snubby watched him in amazement. They themselves a winter or two ago had had to go through the painfully slow process of learning skating the hard way – falling, slipping, bumping down on the ice, scrambling up only to fall again – before they could balance themselves and skate for more than a few metres.

And here was old Barney skating at thirty miles an hour as if he had done nothing but skate all his life long. Look at him now, going round in circles, then shooting off again, then spreading his legs wide and circling once more. What a boy!

"You knew how to skate, you fibber!" shouted Snubby.

"I did not! It's the first time!" called back Barney, his blue eyes gleaming brightly. "It's heavenly – superb – best sport I've ever tried!"

Diana came on the ice just then, also full of astonishment to see Barney skating so easily, Miranda on his shoulder, enjoying this new game to the utmost. Diana was a graceful little skater, and went over to Barney, holding out her hand.

"Skate with me," she said. "That's right, hold my hands like that. Oh, Barney – you skate beautifully!"

It was great fun to be on the ice that clear winter's morning. Roger fell over a lot and groaned, and rubbed himself, quite envious of the others, especially Snubby. Snubby did not skate as gracefully as either Barney or Diana but he was, as usual, full of idiotic tricks, leaping in the air on his skates, twisting himself round in never-ending circles till he fell over in giddiness – and altogether behaving in what Diana called a "very Snubby-ish way."

They had a wonderful morning on the ice, and were glad of the packets of biscuits that Mrs Tickle had given them, which they shared generously with Loony and Miranda.

"Let's skate this afternoon too," said Barney, who felt as if he could never have enough of flying through the frosty air so easily. So the whole day was spent on the pond. It was quite clear of snow now, except at the far end, where trees overhung it and the surface was still snowbound.

They were very tired that evening, so tired that they dragged themselves upstairs very early indeed, immediately after supper. Mrs Tickle was amused – and pleased too, because now she also could get to bed early.

"I don't mind telling you that nothing will make me wake up tonight!" said Snubby, smothering a really enormous yawn.

"A thunderstorm would," said Diana. "It always wakes me."

"No. A thunderstorm wouldn't wake me, nor an earthquake, not even a bomb!" said Snubby.

But he was quite wrong – as wrong as ever he could be!

11

Noise in the Night

Snubby was asleep almost before he had climbed into bed. He felt his eyes closing as he groped for the bedclothes, and then he knew nothing more. He didn't even dream.

The others were almost as sleepy. Even little Miranda was tired out after her day in the frosty air, and snuggled down at the foot of Barney's bed before he was in it. Mrs Tickle was the last of the household to go to sleep.

But she had not been skating for miles all day long. She undressed slowly, folded all her things as she always did, washed herself, and undid her plaited hair to brush it out.

She thought about the four children. Nice children, she said to herself, always willing to give a hand, and always jolly together. But that caution of a Snubby! He was the best of the lot, thought Mrs Tickle, deftly plaiting her long hair again.

"Him and his freckles and jokes! He reminds me of what my Tom used to be –

always up to mischief and as artful as a monkey – yes, as artful as that little Miranda! I didn't take to her at first, but she's got such funny little ways. And that Loony! If ever a dog had the right name, it's him. Taking my clothes and brushes all day long and hiding them."

She was in bed at last, having done all the things she did so meticulously every evening; said her prayers and read her Bible and rubbed cream on her rough hands. She turned out her light and settled down with her hot-water bottle, hugging it to her with pleasure – and then, like the others, she fell fast asleep.

The night was still and the frost was hard. There was not a sound to be heard, for even the owl was too cold to hoot, and flew sadly on his silent wings, looking for mice that he could not see. They were far under the snow, safe in their cosy holes.

And then a thunderous sound split the deep silence – a tremendous noise that echoed through the old house and awoke everyone immediately.

Nobody knew what it was. It had sounded in their dreams, and by the time they had woken, only the echo of the noise was left in their minds.

Snubby leaped up in fright. Diana cowered under the bedclothes. Roger sat up and Barney sprang out of bed. Mrs Tickle covered her head with the bedclothes. "A storm!" she said. "Oh my, what a crash!"

Loony barked madly without stopping, partly with fright but mostly from anger. He had been so sound asleep – not even one ear open – and now this strange noise had woken him without warning.

Roger, who shared a room with Snubby, called across to him: "Snubby, did you hear that crashing noise? What do you suppose it was?"

"The end of the world I should think!" said Snubby, his heart still beating fast. "It can't be a storm – look, you can see the stars in a clear sky."

"I'm going to Diana, to see if she's scared," said Roger, and he got out of bed and ran to Diana's room. He met Barney on the landing.

"Hello. Did you hear that row?" said Roger. "Whatever was it? An explosion of some sort?"

"No. I don't know what it was," said Barney. "I was fast asleep. It sounded pretty near, anyway."

They went into Diana's room. "Diana! Are you all right?" called Roger to his sister. She was still under the bedclothes. She put her head out and blinked at him in the glare of the light.

"Oh, Roger, Barney. Whatever was that?" she said, in a shaky voice.

"Can't imagine – perhaps a peal of thunder," said Roger, speaking cheerfully. He hated Diana to be frightened.

"You needn't worry," said Barney. "The sky isn't stormy – the crash won't come again."

But even as he finished speaking, it did come again. And this time they heard it clearly, not muddled as in a dream.

Rat-a-tat-tat! Rat-a-tat-tat!

The noise echoed all through the house, and then slowly died away. Diana disappeared under the bedclothes with a cry of fright. Roger clutched at Barney.

"The knocker!" he said. "It's someone hammering at the front door with that enormous knocker. Good gracious – who is it coming here in the middle of the night?"

"Perhaps – perhaps it's my father," said Barney. "No, he would have telephoned. Gosh! I really don't feel as if I want to go down and open the door."

They were joined by Mrs Tickle, who, although really too scared to get out of bed, had felt obliged to come and see if the children were all right. She shook so much that she could hardly hold her hands steady.

"What was that?" she said. "Someone knocking at the door? But it's midnight! I'll not open the door. I daren't go down the stairs!"

"I tell you what," said Barney, speaking

as cheerfully as he could, "we'll lean out of the window over the front door and ask who it is. It may be someone who is lost and needing help."

Snubby had now joined them with a very frightened Loony, who produced a string of growls but no barks.

"Why did you say that nothing in the world would wake you tonight, Snubby?" said Diana. "Something always happens when you say silly things like that."

"Come on," said Barney. "Let's go and shout out of the window. Or would you rather stay here with Diana, Mrs Tickle?"

"I'll stay here," said Mrs Tickle. "I'll look after Diana – and she can look after me. And mind, if it's someone lost, don't let them in till you've told me. Waking us all up like this at midnight! It's disgraceful!"

The three boys, with Loony and Miranda, went along the landing to the big window that overlooked the front door. They opened it with difficulty, for it was very stiff.

Outside lay the thick snow, and the snow-man and the snow house loomed up dimly in the bright starlight. Barney leaned out of the window, trying to see down to the front door.

"Who's there?" he shouted. "Who's there?"

They all held their breath to listen for the answer. But none came. There was not a

sound from below. Barney shouted again.

"Who knocked on the door? Answer, please!"

But still there was no answer. The night was silent and still. Barney shut the window, for the air was bitterly cold. He shivered.

"Nobody there," he said. "Not a sound to be heard."

"Do you think we'd better go down and open the door – just in case?" said Roger.

"In case of what?" said Barney, fastening the window.

"Well, in case there's somebody ill there, or exhausted with being lost," said Roger.

"Anyone who can hammer at that knocker with such fury can't be ill or faint," said Barney grimly. "And we don't go down! That's quite certain."

They went back to Mrs Tickle and Diana. "Nobody's there," said Barney briefly.

Mrs Tickle began to shiver again, partly with fright and partly with cold. "It's that Mr No One," she said. "The one that used to come all those years ago and hammer on the door to warn the family that there was a traitor inside."

"Nonsense!" said Roger. "Rubbish! Fiddlesticks! That's a silly old legend. Anyway, there isn't a traitor of any sort or kind in this house, Mrs Tickle. I think it's someone playing a fat-headed joke on us."

"Well, if that's so, we're not going to fall for it," said Barney firmly, though he felt very doubtful indeed that it was a joke. "We're going to go back to bed and get warm and go to sleep and in the morning we'll do a little exploring for footprints up to the front door. Our Mr No One had to go up those steps, and we'll at least see what his feet are like – big – small – middle-size."

"Yes. That's a good idea," said Snubby. "Come on then – let's go to bed."

"I'm going to sleep on the couch in your

room, Diana," said Mrs Tickle. "We'll be company for each other. You'd like that, wouldn't you?"

"Oh, yes," said Diana, and kind Mrs Tickle went off to collect her bedclothes and hot-water bottle, and then made her bed up on the little couch at the other side of Diana's room. Diana felt very comforted to know that she was there and Mrs Tickle was also glad to have Diana's company. That Mr No One – what a fright he had given them all!

Snubby and Roger talked things over for a few minutes and then Snubby fell fast asleep again. Barney, in the next room, puzzled over the knocking for some time, and over the curious fact that nobody was at the door. He didn't for one moment believe in the old legend.

"We'll find out a few things tomorrow morning," he thought, turning over comfortably. "Oh, sorry, Miranda – did I squash you?"

The little monkey had been so frightened by the noise that she had crept right to the bottom of Barney's bed and cuddled by his feet.

The clock down the hall chimed the half hour – half past midnight, thought Barney. Well, look out, Mr Knocker, whoever you are – we'll all be on your trail tomorrow morning!

12

The Footprints

Everyone but Mrs Tickle slept soundly for the rest of the night. Mrs Tickle, who had not tired herself out with vigorous skating, as the children had, was not as sleepy as they were, and she lay and worried about the strange knocking for a long time.

At a quarter to seven she slid off the couch in Diana's room, put on her dressing-gown, and opened the door quietly to go to her own room. It was time to get dressed and go down and see to the lighting of the fires.

Later on, Barney went into Roger's room to dress with him and Snubby and to talk about the night's alarm. They none of them felt scared now; they felt brave and rather scornful of last night's fears. Outside was the brilliant sunshine and the dazzling snow, and the thought of skating and tobogganing drove away the alarms of the night.

In a little while, Diana came knocking at the door. "Are you ready to go down to breakfast? I'm dressed. And I'm hungry!"

"Yes, we're ready," said Roger, opening the door. "I vote we go and have a squint at the knocker that was used so vigorously last night."

So, with Loony streaking ahead of them, the first thing they did was to race down the wide stairs, and go straight to the front door.

"We've not used this door since we first came," said Barney. "We came in this way when we arrived, but ever since then we've used the side door to go in and out."

"We haven't had any fall of snow since we came," said Roger, considering. "So let's think now – about footprints. We drove up in the car to the stone steps that run up to the door . . ."

"So there should only be the marks of the car tyres in the drive and our footmarks going up the steps to the door," said Barney. "And that means, there should now be another set of footprints – Mr No One's – coming up the drive right to these steps, where they will unfortunately be muddled with ours. My word, isn't the door difficult to open!"

It certainly was. It had two great bolts, one at the top and one at the bottom, two locks and a heavy chain. The locks were stiff to turn, but at last they clicked and the children were able to open the great door.

"We've never even seen the knocker yet!" said Diana, and she looked to see what it was like.

It was magnificent. It was in the shape of a great lion's head, and to use it one iron lock of its mane had to be grasped in order to lift the knocker. Diana and the others marvelled at it. They had never seen such a knocker in their lives – no wonder it made so much noise!

"I'll just feel it to see how heavy it is," said Snubby, and took hold of the handle made by the lock of the lion's mane. He raised the knocker, but it was so heavy that it fell back again immediately.

Crash!

Loony fell down the steps in fright, and Miranda shot under Barney's jumper. Diana jumped violently and turned on Snubby at once. "*Don't!* I can't bear being made to jump like that. Why must you be so silly?"

"Sorry," said Snubby, very much startled himself. "I'd no idea it was so heavy."

Mrs Tickle came running into the hall, looking as scared as could be. "What . . ." she began, and then saw the children standing there. "Oh, bless us all, I thought it was that Mr No One again. I was just coming to give him a piece of my mind."

"It was only me," said Snubby. "Sorry! My word, isn't it an enormous knocker, Mrs Tickle. No wonder it gave us all a fright last night. Whoever knocked must have been a strong fellow, to crash it on the door like that."

"Well, don't you do that again, or the breakfast will be spoiled," said Mrs Tickle, still rather cross. "I dropped an egg I was holding and it splashed all over my shoe – look!"

"Loony, lick it!" ordered Snubby, but before the dog could get to the shoe, Miranda was there, licking the egg yolk with much enjoyment.

"How can you, Miranda!" said Diana, in disgust.

"Let's look for footprints," said Roger, and he went to the top of the steps and looked down.

There was not much help to be got from the mass of footprints there, not from those just in front of the door, under the porch. A jumble of footmarks flattened the thick snow, and it was difficult to tell one from another.

"We all stood here together when we arrived," said Diana. "Your father, Barney, and we four – and Loony of course leaping about everywhere – but we shan't find Miranda's tiny paw-marks because she was on your shoulder."

"There'll be marks of the suitcases too," said Barney. "Yes, you can see them here and there."

They all went down the steps, trying to keep to the sides, so that they did not make any further prints to confuse those already there. It was when they came to the bottom of the steps and into the drive that they really discovered something.

The marks of the car tyres were there, of course, coming up the drive, and stopping by the door – then swinging round and back when Mr Martin drove off again. But there was a strange line of footprints, all by itself, coming right across the drive from the snow-clad lawn nearby. The children followed them to where they themselves had made hundreds of prints when they snowballed one another.

"Look at these!" said Barney, in excitement. "These prints aren't made by us –

they're enormous! They are made by someone wearing really big boots. They look like wellington boots, many sizes larger than ours."

The children looked down at them earnestly. Yes, these prints were not theirs. What a pity they were lost in the jumble of footmarks they themselves had made, and could not be followed any further. They thought they could make them out here and there, but it was very uncertain.

"Let's follow them back to the front door," said Roger. "Everyone's got to be jolly careful not to tread on them or spoil them."

They followed them across the lawn and over the drive to the bottom of the steps, where, of course, they were lost in a jumble of others.

Mrs Tickle came to the front door, looking rather impatient. "Aren't you ever coming for breakfast?" she said. "And do you want to catch your death of cold, messing about outside without even a coat on?"

"Mrs Tickle, come and look; we've found Mr No One's footprints!" called Snubby. "Do come!"

Mrs Tickle pricked up her ears at once. She went cautiously down the front-entrance steps, afraid of slipping, and was proudly shown the set of prints leading up to the bottom step.

"Follow us and we'll show you where they came from," said Roger, and took her to where they had had their snowball fight. "See, they are lost here – but Mr No One went over the lawn from here, right across the drive, and then he must have gone up the steps to knock on the door."

"Yes," said Mrs Tickle, looking extremely puzzled. "Yes, but why is there only one set of prints?"

"Because he was by himself!" said Snubby, thinking that Mrs Tickle was not very clever.

"Yes, I know that. But why isn't there a set of prints leading back from the front-door steps?" said Mrs Tickle. "I mean – he'd got to walk back, hadn't he? And there are no footmarks showing that he walked away again."

Nobody had thought of that at all. How very stupid! Barney frowned, very puzzled. "Yes, we didn't think of that – we were so excited at finding strange footmarks that we never thought that there should be two sets; one coming and one going."

"This is horrid," said Diana. "How can anyone come to our front door and knock, and then not go away? He's not standing there now! Then how did he go away?"

"For goodness sake come and have your breakfast," said Mrs Tickle, shivering in the cold. "I'll have you all in bed with bad chills if you stay out here any longer. Leave Mr No One and his antics to himself and come away in."

They obeyed her, very silent. It certainly was very, very strange that there were no footmarks going away from the house – only one set, walking towards it! How did Mr No One, as they all called the night visitor, go away if he didn't use his feet? It was a puzzle – a real mystery!

They sat down to breakfast, and helped themselves to hot porridge. Snubby remembered the fright he had had two nights before when he thought he had seen someone standing near the snow house while they were having their supper. He reminded the others.

"I bet that was Mr No One too," he said. "And I bet that's his glove we found!"

"Oh, yes," said Roger. "I expect it was. Well, we now know he was a man with large hands and large feet and he has probably got one odd navy glove. But what we don't know is why on earth he's messing about at Rat-a-Tat House."

"I wish he'd go somewhere else," said Diana, pouring out large cups of milky coffee for everyone. "And I hope to goodness he doesn't come knocking at our front door again."

"Do you think we'd better phone my father and tell him about it?" said Barney.

"After all, this is my granny's house, and if anyone intends to burgle it, we ought to do something about it."

"Yes, of course. We'll phone and tell the whole tale," said Roger. "Good idea. Perhaps your father will come over and have a fight with Mr No One, Barney."

But when they went to telephone, there was no dialling tone. The snow had brought down the wires, and until they were mended Rat-a-Tat house was completely cut off from everywhere!

13

A Few Interesting Things

"Well!" said Barney, hanging up the telephone receiver. "That's it. We're cut off
from everyone at the moment. Couldn't even
get a doctor if we wanted one."

"We could get to the village of Boffame
somehow, if we had to," said Roger.

"It would take us ages," said Barney. "All
through that thick snow! I bet we'd get lost,
too. All the countryside looks alike when it's
covered with snow. We'd need skis to make
any headway."

"So we'll have to solve the mystery of
Rat-a-Tat House by ourselves!" said Snubby,
cheerfully. "Oh, well, we're jolly good at
mysteries, I think. We've had four already –
the Rockingdown Mystery, the Rilloby Fair
Mystery . . ."

"The Rubadub Mystery," said Diana,
"and what was the other? Oh, yes, the Ring
o' Bells Mystery."

"We'll call this the Rat-a-Tat Mystery
then, as Snubby said," put in Barney. "How

weird – they all begin with R."

"Is there any more bacon and eggs?" asked Snubby, hopefully.

"Certainly not," said Diana indignantly. "You've had twice as much as anyone else."

"Oooh, I haven't. Have I, Loony?" said Snubby, looking hurt. Loony thumped his tail on the ground and licked Snubby's hand.

"Stop thumping," ordered Diana. "I don't want to hear any knocking or thumping or hammering for ages. Loony, stop it!"

"Does anyone feel like tobogganing today?" asked Roger. "My legs feel quite all right now."

Barney would have liked to skate all day long, but when the others voted for tobogganing he nodded too.

"Right," said Roger. "That's settled then. But don't let's choose such a steep hill for our tobogganing this time – it really is such a drag up."

So they chose another hill, and dragged their toboggans up joyfully, after they had done all they could to help a rather silent Mrs Tickle. She wasn't at all happy about Mr No One!

When they came to the top they had a fine view over the white countryside, and suddenly saw something they had not been able to see from the other hill they had tobogganed down.

"What's that?" said Snubby, pointing to what looked like a small house, whose roof was white with snow. It stood very close to one bank of the lake and, in fact, looked almost as if it were on the lake.

Everyone looked down at it. "It's a boat-house, of course!" said Roger. "Built partly on land and partly over water. There'll be boats in there, won't there, Barney?"

"Yes," said Barney, remembering that his father had told him that boats were stored for use on the lake in the summer. "I'd forgotten there was a boat-house. We might go and explore it when we're tired of tobogganing."

The snow was beautifully crisp for tobogganing again and the children really enjoyed themselves – especially when Snubby went down the hill alone with Loony and the toboggan struck something, leaped in the air and flung both Snubby and Loony into the snow. Poor Loony fell in so deep that he was lost to sight!

"Loony, Loony, where are you?" yelled Snubby in a panic. "Come and help, you asses, don't stand laughing your heads off there. Loony will suffocate in the snow."

"Not Loony!" shouted Roger. "He's having a nice little rest!"

Loony was, in fact, tunnelling under the snow, too out of breath even to bark. He popped up just by Snubby and made him jump. He leaped on him in delight and over went poor Snubby, deeper in the snow than ever, with Loony leaping about on top of him. The others laughed till they ached, but Snubby was most annoyed.

"Let's eat our morning biscuits in the boat-house – if we can get in," said Barney when they began to feel tired and hungry. So they went over the snow to the boat-house, which, with its white-painted walls and snow-clad roof, was really quite difficult to see from a distance.

It was shut and locked. "Blast!" said Barney. "We can't get in."

They went to look in at a window, and saw three boats there, in the dimness of the shed. Snubby wandered right round the shed and then suddenly shouted: "Hey, here's a broken window. We can get in after all."

The others went round to him, but before he came to the broken window, Roger suddenly saw something else. Footmarks! Large ones, very much the same size as those they had seen on the drive.

"I say, we're on to something now," said Barney, excited. "Perhaps our Mr No One lives here – trespassing in my father's boat-house. Anyone got a torch?"

No one had, which was a pity. Barney looked at the broken window and saw that he could easily get in without tearing his clothes. "I'll just have a snoop round," he

said, and was up on the windowsill easily and in at the jagged window.

The others waited eagerly. He soon came back with a bit of news. "Yes, I think our Mr No One is staying here. One of the boats is lined with boat cushions, as if someone sleeps there. And I found an empty cigarette packet. Look!"

He gave the packet to Roger and then climbed deftly out of the window. Yes, Mr No One used the window to get in by, that was certain. Now, where did the footmarks go? They might lead to Mr No One himself!

But the prints merely went to the front of the boat-house, which, instead of standing on piles in the water, as it usually did, was now standing in thick ice, for the lake was frozen. A soon as the footprints reached the ice, they disappeared, of course, for no footprints showed on the ice.

"At least the footprints go both ways this time," said Roger thankfully. "Look, there are sets leading up to the window and sets leading away again – all jumbled up, but clear enough to see that the fellow came and went."

"Who is he – a tramp?" wondered Diana. "But why would a tramp come and knock at Rat-a-Tat House? And, anyway, how did he make footprints that only led there – and not away? That's been puzzling me all day!"

"Oh, let's not worry about that," said Snubby, who had finished his biscuits and wanted to toboggan again. "Come on – it's cold just standing here."

They were all bright-eyed and red-cheeked when they went in for lunch, feeling quite ravenous.

"Has Mr No One been knocking at the door again?" asked Snubby cheerfully, as Mrs Tickle brought in a dishful of chops surrounded by fried potatoes and peas. "Oh, I say – look at that! It makes me feel hungrier than ever."

"That Mr No One wouldn't dare to come in the daytime," said Mrs Tickle. "I've got my rolling-pin ready, and a kettle boiling on the stove. I'm ready for him if he comes banging at any door, front or back."

They all laughed at the determined little woman. She laughed too. "There you are – you get on with your lunch – and there's a big treacle pudding to follow so leave a bit of room for that."

It was a lovely meal as usual, and the children felt lazy after it. But the day was again so beautiful that no one wanted a long rest. Soon they were on their way to toboggan again and spent the whole afternoon racing down and climbing up the snowy hills. They were very tired when they dragged themselves back to Rat-a-Tat House just as it was getting dusk.

"I can't find enough strength to throw a snowball at anyone," said Snubby sorrowfully. "As for Loony, he's so tired I'm having to drag him back on my toboggan, the lazy fellow."

"Our snowman is still standing guard over our snow house," said Roger. "Hello, Mr Icy-Cold. Your hat's gone crooked. Let me put it straight for you."

He tipped the old hat straight, and they all went on to the garden door to take off their wet boots and gloves. Mrs Tickle heard them and came to welcome them.

"You're late," she said. "I've had hot buttered toast keeping warm for you for twenty minutes. Hurry up and wash, or the toast will be cold."

"I can't even hurry for buttered toast," said Snubby. "I'm an old, old man, Mrs Tickle, bent and stooping, and my legs will hardly bear me. Oh, what tobogganing does to you!"

"Go on with you," said Mrs Tickle. "Bent old man you may be, but you'll eat more than your share of the toast, I'll be bound!"

They all sat at the laden white-clothed table, enjoying their meal, with Diana pouring out huge cups of tea for everyone. They were happy but so tired that they could hardly tease one another. Loony flopped down under the table with an enormous sigh. He was very much afraid he would go to sleep before the titbits began to arrive for him below the table.

"Let's draw the curtains," said Barney. "I don't want to feel that Mr No One is hiding in our snow house again and watching us while we eat."

Barney got up to draw them. Before he pulled them across the window, he looked out into the darkness, pierced only by the rays of the bright lamp. He swung round suddenly. "I say! Our snowman's gone! He's not there!"

"Gone! But he can't be! Why, he was there when we came in, half an hour ago!" said Diana. "Roger put his hat straight."

"Well, he's not there now," said Barney. "Come and see. You can just make out the snow house – but no snowman! Gosh! What extraordinary things are happening? Where has Mr Icy-Cold gone?"

14

Another Mystery

The four children really were astounded at the disappearance of their snowman, especially as they had passed him such a short time ago on their way back to tea.

"Someone must have knocked him down," said Barney at last. "It's the only explanation. Snowmen don't walk away on their own – not even our nice Mr Icy-Cold."

"Well, shall we get a torch and go out and see if he's been knocked down and made into just a heap of snow?" said Roger.

"Yes. And we may perhaps see the person who spoiled him," said Barney, getting his torch off the mantelpiece. "We'll take Loony too; he'll soon smell out anyone hiding nearby, watching to see if we've noticed the disappearance of the snowman."

"I don't really see any point in knocking him down," began Diana, really puzzled, and then she stopped.

A cry had come from the kitchen, and then the children heard hurried footsteps running down the passage to the sitting-room. The door was flung open, and there was Mrs Tickle "all of a shake" again.

"What's the matter?" cried Barney.

"The snowman! Your snowman! He came and peeped in at the kitchen window when I was having my tea," panted Mrs Tickle. The children stared at her unbelievingly.

"But Mrs Tickle, you must know that a snowman doesn't walk!" said Roger. "It must have been a—"

"I tell you, it was your snowman, all white, and with that hat on," said Mrs Tickle, sinking down into a chair. "Such goings-on! We'll get back to Little Wendleman as soon as possible. You phone your father, Barney."

"The phone is out of order," said Barney, and Mrs Tickle groaned. Then she looked out of the window and gave a little scream.

"He's gone – your snowman's gone!" she said. "I thought it was him, peering in at my window and frightening the life out of me. Hat and all."

This was really very puzzling. None of the children believed for a moment that it was actually their snowman that Mrs Tickle had seen. But who was it? And why was he all in white? And how was it that their own snowman had disappeared so very suddenly?

"I believe that wasn't a snowman at all, out there," said Mrs Tickle, nodding her head towards the window. "He may have been once, but after that it was someone covered in snow, watching us."

"Oh, no, Mrs Tickle!" said Barney. "Honestly, we walked close by him this morning and this afternoon, and there is no doubt at all that he was a snowman made of snow. Why, Roger even put his hat on straight for him. Didn't you, Roger?"

"Well, then – you explain to me how he walked away and came and looked in the kitchen window," said Mrs Tickle fiercely. "You tell me that!"

They couldn't. It was as much a puzzle to them as to poor Mrs Tickle. Barney and Roger went out to the kitchen with her to see if the snowman was still doing some peeping. But he wasn't. Barney took his torch into the backyard and shone it everywhere, but there was nothing to be seen, except a jumble of footmarks all mixed up together – obviously Mrs Tickle's and some of theirs. It was impossible to tell if there were any others as well.

They came back and Mrs Tickle firmly locked and bolted the door behind her. "I won't have that snowman walking into my kitchen," she said.

"It's a pity he doesn't," said Snubby. "He would go and warm himself at your big fire, Mrs Tickle, and in a few minutes all you'd have to do would be to mop up a big pool of water, and empty the snowman down the sink."

Mrs Tickle had to laugh. "You're a real caution, you are," she said. "Have you finished your tea yet?"

"Gosh, no!" said Snubby, quite shocked to think that he could have left his tea and forgotten about it. "I was in the middle of my third piece of buttered toast."

"You'd better go back and finish it, then," said Mrs Tickle, giving him a little push.

The children went back to the sitting-room to finish their tea. They all felt rather excited, but they found it difficult to believe that Mrs Tickle had seen anyone really like a snowman. It must have been a trick of the dusk.

"But that doesn't solve our problem – of why our snowman suddenly disappeared," said Snubby.

"He might have melted," suggested Diana. "The weather might have got warmer. It feels like it."

"You can't possibly tell what the weather's like sitting in this hot room," said Roger. "I'm sure it's as cold as ever. I hope it is, anyway. I want to go skating again tomorrow."

"Yes!" said Barney, beaming. "Yes, let's all go skating."

They had a very pleasant evening with no

more disturbances. They thought that Mrs Tickle seemed a bit scared of being in the kitchen by herself, so they decided to ask her to come and have a game of Snap-Grab with them – that would cheer her up, and make her forget the snowman who had peeped in at her window.

They set the cork in the middle of the table and Roger dealt the cards. Whenever anyone saw that two cards were the same, he not only had to call "Snap!" but had to grab the cork as well. This saved a great many arguments as to who it was had called "Snap" first! Snubby grabbed at the cork so fiercely every time he called "Snap" that they made him go and fetch his gloves and put one on.

"You've scratched my hand twice," complained Diana. "You really are rough at this game, Snubby. I shan't play unless you wear a glove."

So Snubby fetched his gloves and put one on his right hand. Now, when he grabbed the cork, he couldn't scratch anyone!

Miranda loved a game of Snap and kept trying to grab the cork herself when anyone yelled "Snap!" Once she really did get hold of it and leaped away to the mantelpiece with it, holding it so tightly that Barney couldn't get it away from her.

"You really are naughty," he said, but Miranda refused to give up the cork. She put it into her mouth and held it there, looking wickedly at Barney.

Snubby laughed. He got up and put a few old cards on the mantelpiece beside Miranda.

"Here you are," he said. "You can have a game of Snap all to yourself, cork and all, you little wretch! We've got another cork in the card-box."

Miranda picked up the cards in delight, and began to chatter to herself. She took the cork out of her mouth as soon as Barney was safely settled again at the table, and set it down beside her. Then she began to deal out the cards.

"Look! Do look at Miranda!" said Diana, amused. "She'll be yelling out "Snap!" in a minute."

But she didn't get as far as that, of course! She did, however, think that it would be more fun to play with someone, rather than by herself, and in a few minutes she leaped off the mantelpiece, cork in mouth, and cards in one paw. She scuttled along the floor to where Loony was lying in a deep sleep under the table, and woke him by biting his tail.

She dealt out the cards and put the cork on the floor. Diana, peeping under the table, went off into fits of laughter and Barney produced his uproarious laugh, that always set everyone else laughing too.

Loony wasn't at all pleased. He sniffed at the cork, looked scornfully at the cards and once more went to sleep. Miranda had to play on her own again.

Snubby soon had all the cards, as usual, though Mrs Tickle ran him very close. She was surprisingly good at grabbing the cork, much to Snubby's annoyance. It was, in fact, a very jolly evening, despite the upsets of two or three hours before.

"Bedtime," said Mrs Tickle at last. "And let's hope Mr No One doesn't come hammering at the door again. If he does, I don't stir out of my bed. Let him knock all he likes."

"I'll second that," said Roger, yawning. "Yes, let's go to bed. Diana's nearly asleep already."

They turned out the lights, collected Loony and Miranda (who still clutched her cards and cork), and set off upstairs. In half an hour's time the house was in darkness, and everyone was sound asleep, except Loony.

It is true that Loony was asleep, but tonight he had one ear open, which meant that one ear was awake, and so Loony was not really sound asleep. The upsets of the night before, and the excitement over the snowman had put him on his guard. He meant to keep one ear awake all night – just in case!

It was just about midnight when that one ear heard something unusual – not the crashing of the knocker on the front door this time but a small sound, somewhere downstairs. Loony's ear took in the noise, and he awoke at once and sat up. Snubby was lost in a deep sleep, and took no notice. Loony ran to the door and listened.

Yes, something was going on downstairs. He ran to Snubby, and gave a little warning growl. Then he pawed at him. Finally he jumped on Snubby's middle – that always awoke him, as Loony very well knew.

It awoke him now and he sat up indignantly. "Ass! What did you want to do that for? Haven't I told you . . . I say – what are you growling for?"

Loony's growl put Snubby on his guard at

once. Perhaps someone was about to crash that knocker again and Loony had heard footsteps. Right – Snubby would go down and watch for Mr No One, and catch him hammering at that knocker.

"Come on," said Snubby. "Something's up!"

15

Look Out, Snubby!

Snubby slipped on his dressing-gown and looked across at Roger, shining his torch on him. He was fast asleep. Should he wake him? No, he would go down and pry around a little first, and then if there was anything exciting, he could come back and get Roger.

Loony was still growling in a low tone, his hackles up and his body stiff. There was no doubt that he could hear something going on.

Snubby began to feel excited. "Adventures in the night!" he whispered to Loony. "Come on, old fellow."

They went out of the room quietly, and Snubby shut the door behind him. They crept along the wide landing, and came to the top of the stairs. Snubby shut off his torch and listened. He could hear sounds now – muffled sounds. He thought they came from the kitchen.

"Who's there?" he wondered. "Mr No

One perhaps! Loony, we'd better go carefully. Gosh! It might be the snowman, of course. I never thought of that."

Snubby would never have dreamed of thinking he might really meet a snowman, if it been broad daylight – but somehow, in the dark, silent house, with strange sounds going on, it seemed quite possible that he might meet the snowman round the next corner. He tightened his dressing-gown belt, and went softly down the stairs, torch in hand.

Yes, the sounds quite definitely came from the kitchen. They were curious sounds, and Snubby couldn't quite make them out. There were bumps and scraping noises and grunts as if someone was carrying something heavy. What could be happening?

Snubby came to the bottom of the stairs and went down the hall towards the big kitchen door. Mrs Tickle always left it open at night, but now it was shut. Snubby crept towards it, Loony close at his heels, still growling very softly.

Snubby put his eye to the keyhole, but the kitchen was in darkness, except for what seemed to him to be a ray from a stationary torch. He heard a low voice, and then a bump from the far side of the kitchen. Snubby tried to think what was just there – was it the larder? No. Was it the cupboard where Mrs Tickle kept the crockery and pans? No. Of course – it was the cellar! He and Barney had noticed the door there, and had tried to open it, to see where it led to, but it had been locked.

"The cellar's locked, and I don't know where the key is," Mrs Tickle had told them. "I expect your granny has something stored down there, Barney. It was open when I was here last summer – your cousins were here boating and swimming. I expect your granny locked it when we all went home."

But whoever was in the kitchen now had evidently got hold of the key to the cellar, because Snubby, straining his ears, could quite well hear someone going down the steps. What in the world was happening? Were thieves robbing the cellar of any goods stored there? What a time to choose – in the middle of a snowy spell, when there was no chance of a lorry or van to take them away.

Loony continued to growl, and Snubby got tired of looking through the keyhole. He suddenly decided that he would slip out of the garden door and go round to the kitchen window. He would have a much better view there.

"Come on," he whispered to Loony, and they went back up the hall together. They passed the open sitting-room door and, in the light of the dying fire, Loony suddenly caught sight of the gleaming eyes of the bearskin rug. He backed heavily into Snubby and growled loudly.

"Look out!" whispered Snubby, almost falling over. "What's the matter? Oh, it's the old bear. My word, doesn't he look lifelike tonight!"

He was about to go on when a sudden idea struck him. Why shouldn't he drape the bearskin over him and pull the head over his – if the men happened to see him looking in at the kitchen window, they would have the fright of their lives to see what appeared to be a live bear!

"Also," thought Snubby, shivering, "it would be nice and warm to wear. I expect it will be terribly cold outside."

All thoughts of waking Roger went from his mind and he felt a tingling feeling run down his back as a tremendous excitement suddenly took hold of him. Yes, he would wear the bearskin. He would give those thieves a fright, and he would find out what they were doing. What a tale to tell the others! Snubby's chest swelled in pride, and he patted Loony on the head.

"I'm going to wear the bearskin," he whispered. "So don't get excited about it. The bear won't eat me!"

And then, to Loony's everlasting amazement, Snubby went to the bearskin, lifted it up, and draped it round his shoulders with the big head on top of his! When he bent his own head the bear's head flopped lower and it looked exactly as if it were alive.

It was very heavy – heavier than Snubby had imagined. But he was quite determined to wear it! Loony gaped at him, his tail well down. He couldn't understand this at all, and he was ready to leap on the bearskin if it showed any signs of biting Snubby or clawing him.

Snubby went slowly to the garden door, weighed down by the skin over his shoulders. He unlocked the door and he and Loony went out into the cold, frosty night. The snow was thick and deep as he went round the house to the kitchen entrance, Loony obediently at his heels.

The spaniel growled as they came near the kitchen door, and Snubby tapped him on the head. It was essential that the men should not hear anything. As they rounded the corner, they saw that the kitchen door was open – and, to Snubby's amazement, some hefty boxes, about the size of small trunks, were piled in the little kitchen yard.

He stared at them. They were only very dimly outlined in the starlight, for there was no moon, and Snubby could not make out anything at all except their size. What were the men doing with them – hiding them in the cellar?

"Or perhaps taking them out!" thought

Snubby. "Yes, of course – they *are* taking them out. That's why the cellar door was locked and the key was gone. These men must have come to the house while it stood empty and hidden something in the cellar, knowing it would be safe in an empty house, with nobody to pry and peep."

He stole past the boxes to the kitchen window and peered inside, just as the snow-man was supposed to have looked in at Mrs Tickle that evening. A torch lay on a table, its beam pointing towards the cellar door – which, of course, was open.

Loony did his best to peer through the window too, putting his paws on the sill. He almost choked himself trying not to bark – especially when a man appeared at the top of the cellar steps, going backwards as if he were helping another man to carry something heavy.

Snubby watched in excitement. Yes, it was another box – very heavy too. Goodness gracious, no wonder the men had locked the cellar door and taken the key! Mrs Tickle would have been amazed to find the cellar full of heavy boxes! Snubby supposed that the men hadn't had time to remove them before Mrs Tickle and the rest of them came down to Rat-a-Tat House – they must have thought that the house would certainly stand empty all the winter.

The first man came right out of the cellar followed by a second man; they carried a big box between them.

"Put it down for a moment, Jim," said the second man, panting. He was fat, as Snubby could see in the light of the torch that lay on the nearby table, but he could not see the faces of the men at all.

Loony could bear this no longer. He suddenly gave a terrific growl and the startled men turned to the window at once, one of them flashing a torch there. He almost dropped it when he saw a great bear's head, apparently looking in at them with gleaming, staring eyes – and, much lower down, just above the sill, another furry head, black this time, with another pair of gleaming eyes!

"Look! What's that? No, it can't be a bear!" said the man called Jim, in a startled voice. "What is it, Stan?"

Snubby dropped down as soon as he saw the men had seen him, and so did Loony. "Quick!" said Snubby. "We must get back to the others, Loony, and wake them up."

He slipped as he shambled along in the deep snow and went down on all fours, looking now for all the world like a real bear. Loony, glancing at him in amazement, half wondered if the bear had eaten Snubby, for there was little to be seen of the boy now.

The two men rushed out of the kitchen door together, shining their torches. They saw the bear shambling along with Loony. One of them took out a gun, but the other motioned him to put it away. "We don't want to rouse the whole household with the sound of a shot," he said. "Besides, somehow I don't think that bear is real."

Poor Snubby didn't know what to do now. If he stood up to get along more quickly, the men would see that it was only someone wearing a bearskin, and not a real bear. On the other hand, he couldn't get along at all fast on all fours in the snow.

The bearskin solved his difficulties by slipping right off his shoulders, and the men at once saw that there was only a small boy on all fours in the snow. They were most relieved. Loony stood by Snubby growling in a most alarming way, ready to fly at the men at the word from the boy.

"Get up," said the man called Jim, to Snubby. "What's the meaning of this foolery?"

"Well," said Snubby indignantly, standing up straight, "I like that! What's the meaning of you delving about in our cellars in the middle of the night?"

"No cheek from you," said the other man roughly. "Get back into the kitchen at once – go on – and the dog too. And I warn you, if that dog begins to bark or try any funny business with his teeth, I'll kick him over the wall."

"No, don't," said Snubby in alarm, looking at the man's great wellington boots. He hitched his dressing-gown round him and went back to the kitchen, glad to be in the warm, for it was freezing hard outside.

His heart was beating fast. What was going to happen now? Something very unpleasant, that was certain.

16

Down in the Cellar

Snubby went over to the fire that was still gleaming in the range, and faced the men. His red hair stood on end, and he felt very scared. But he put on a bold face, and even tried to whistle.

The men stood together, talking in a low voice. Snubby's heart sank. They must be discussing what to do with him, and there were so many unpleasant possibilities! Could he make a dash for it? He eyed the door that led into the hall. He knew that it was locked, but the key was on his side. He might be able to dash over, unlock the door, open it and rush upstairs.

He suddenly made up his mind and raced for the door, putting out his hand to turn the key. But the men were on to him in a flash. Loony, now thoroughly aroused, and eager to defend Snubby, bared his teeth and went for the men, snapping at their legs. But the thick rubber boots they wore went up to their knees and Loony only got mouthfuls of hard rubber. Snubby yelled and slipped between the men, now making for the open door that led into the yard but Jim was there to prevent him.

Then Snubby saw the opened cellar door and ran to that. Down the stone steps he went, falling down the last four, with Loony on top of him. Snubby was up at once, and ran to the farthest corner, fumbling and stumbling in the dark, afraid that the men would be after him down here.

But no – they didn't come down the steps. There was only the thud of the cellar door shutting, and then Snubby heard the turning of the key in the lock.

"Gosh! I've made myself a prisoner," he groaned. "I bet those fellows planned to lock me up here anyhow, while they go off with those boxes – they must be going to take them away somewhere. I wonder if they've got a van. No, how could they in this snow?"

He sat down on an old broken chair, and Loony pressed close to him. He didn't understand this at all. Why had Snubby come down here into this cold dark place? Why didn't he go back to his warm bed and let Loony cuddle against his legs? The spaniel gave a little whine, and Snubby patted his silky head.

"Why did you give that frightfully fierce growl when we were looking in at the

window, Loony," he groaned. "It was all because of that that we got caught. Honestly, you really are a loony dog!"

Snubby listened to see if there were any more noises upstairs. He rubbed his bruises and decided to go up to the locked cellar door and see if he could hear anything useful. So up he went, Loony pressing behind.

He could hear low voices, but could not make out a word. "They're moving the box they put down in the kitchen," he thought. "Putting it outside with the others, I expect. What's in them, I wonder? And where are they going to put them? I might have found out all that if I'd been more sensible – or if Loony had."

It was so cold and draughty at the top of the stone steps that Snubby went down to the cellar again.

"Looks as if we've got to spend the night here, Loony," he said miserably. "Blast! Why didn't I wake Roger and let him come too? He'll go on sleeping all night long, and it won't be until Mrs Tickle comes down to the kitchen in the morning that anyone will hear me yelling. Brrrrrr! It's cold here!"

He flashed his torch round the cellar. It was very big and rambling. Shelves ran up to the ceiling here and there, and were laden with all kinds of stores, especially tinned food. Snubby stared at the labels – pineapple, peaches, pears, grapefruit – his mouth watered. What a pity he hadn't a tin-opener with him.

There was an old wringer there, and various broken chairs stood in corners. A space had evidently been cleared for the boxes, and Snubby could see where they had stood for they had left their outlines in the dust.

He shivered. What a horrid cold place this was. "Loony, let's see if we can find something a bit warmer than the stone floor to lie on," he said, and he and the spaniel went round the big cellar poking into everything.

They made a good find at last – an old mattress, rolled up and tied with rope. "Good!" said Snubby. "Got a knife to cut the rope, Loony?"

Loony wagged his tail, knowing this was a joke. Snubby had no knife, of course, in his dressing-gown, so he had to struggle with the knots. He got them undone at last and the mattress unrolled itself. Snubby lay down on it, gathered his dressing-gown round him and cuddled Loony, who was better than any hot-water bottle!

"Now we'll try and go to sleep, and hope that Mrs Tickle will hear me yelling in the morning," he said. But it took him a long time to fall asleep. For one thing, he was very excited, and for another he was very cold. But he did sleep at last, Loony curled up against him as close as possible.

Nobody knew that Snubby was not in his bed. Upstairs, the rest of the party slept soundly, the three children tired out with their day's sport. Mrs Tickle heard no sound either, and hardly stirred in her bed till the alarm clock went off and woke her.

She got up, dressed and went downstairs. The kitchen fire was still in, thank goodness, so she only had to rake the embers together and put on some coal. Then she took her brooms and dusters and set off to get the sitting-room clean and tidy, and to light the fire there.

She was most astonished to find the bearskin rug gone. She stood and stared at the empty place where it usually lay and wondered what had happened to it.

"It's that dog Loony," she decided. "He must have come down in the night and taken it off somewhere. Where has he put it? What a dog! I can't leave a duster or brush about anywhere but what he's off and away with them. I'll have to tie them all round my waist soon. Where can he have taken that bearskin rug?"

She didn't hear poor Snubby yelling in the cellar, because the sitting-room was a good way from the kitchen. She finished cleaning it and then went to mop and dust the hall.

Upstairs Roger was awake, and rather surprised to see Snubby's bed empty and Loony gone too. "He must have dressed and gone out early," he thought. "No, he hasn't; his clothes are still there. Perhaps he's in Barney's room."

He went to see, but Snubby wasn't there either, of course. Barney was already half dressed, looking forward to another day of skating. Roger looked round the room in surprise.

"Isn't Snubby here?" he said. "He's not in our room. His clothes are there, though."

"I bet he's gone down to ask Mrs Tickle for a snack before breakfast," said Barney, and Roger thought that was very likely.

Diana came out of her room, fully dressed, as he went back. "Buck up, Roger!" she said. "I'm going down to help Mrs Tickle." And down she went. Barney followed almost at once. They met Mrs Tickle in the hall, just finishing the polishing.

"Hello, Mrs Tickle!" said Barney. "I hope the old snowman didn't visit you in the night!"

"Go on with you!" said Mrs Tickle. "Are you going to lay the breakfast table for me, Diana, seeing that you're up nice and early?"

"Barney and I will do it together," said Diana, going to the sideboard where the cloths were kept. "Oh, where's the bearskin gone?"

"That dog Loony's taken it, I think," said

Mrs Tickle. "Mad as a hatter, he is."

She went off into the kitchen, and then, a minute later, she came hurrying back, looking puzzled and indignant.

"I went to shake my dusters in the yard," she said, "and bless us all, if the bearskin isn't lying out there in the snow! But how could Loony have taken it through a locked door?"

"Isn't Snubby downstairs?" asked Barney in surprise. "He's not in his room – we thought he'd probably gone down to the kitchen to ask you for a snack. You're sure he's not in the larder, Mrs Tickle?"

Mrs Tickle began to look astonished. "No. I've not seen Snubby or Loony this morning and yet there's the bearskin out in the snow. Perhaps Snubby's playing some joke."

"He's an ass," said Barney impatiently. "What can he be up to? He must be somewhere in the kitchen, Mrs Tickle – hiding for some reason of his own."

Diana, Barney and Mrs Tickle went back to the kitchen, and Roger, coming downstairs, joined them. As soon as they were inside the room, they stopped in surprise. From somewhere came a voice – Snubby's voice – yelling loudly. And with it came a hammering on the other side of the cellar door.

"Help! Help! Open the cellar door. Help!

Mrs Tickle, are you there? Help!"

"Good gracious! It's Snubby – down in the cellar, of all places," said Barney, and ran to the door.

"But it's locked," said Mrs Tickle. "And there's no key to it, you remember. How could Snubby get in? And look – there's no key now."

Barney was at the cellar door, tugging at the handle. "Snubby! Why are you in there? Where's the key? It's not this side."

"Oh, they've taken it with them, the beasts!" said Snubby, with a groan. "I might have guessed. Can you break the door down, Barney?"

Everyone was astounded to know that Snubby was locked in the cellar! And who were "the beasts" who had apparently taken the key – a key that hadn't been there before, as Mrs Tickle very well knew.

"Try the key of the kitchen door, or of the door into the hall," said Diana, suddenly remembering that the keys at home were often interchangeable. "Quick, Roger, get them. Snubby must be freezing cold in there."

Roger got the two keys, and oh, what a bit of luck – the kitchen door key fitted the cellar lock! He turned it and out came poor Snubby, with Loony barking madly at his heels.

17

Barney Thinks Things Out

"Snubby! How did you get in there?"

"What happened? Gosh, you look cold!"

"Come over to the fire, Snubby; your hands are like ice."

Everyone spoke at once, and Diana dragged the shivering Snubby to the fire, which was now blazing well. Mrs Tickle was simply amazed that he should have been in the cellar all night. Whatever next!

Snubby got as close to the fire as he could and held his hands out to the flames thankfully. "My word, it was cold down in the cellar," he said. "If I hadn't had Loony for a hot-water bottle I'd have been frozen stiff."

"But, Snubby, how did you get locked in there? What were you doing, wandering about at night!" cried Mrs Tickle.

"I had an adventure," said Snubby, beginning to feel pleasantly warm, and very much the centre of attention. "Loony woke me in the middle of the night. I heard a noise and came down to see what it was . . ."

"Snubby, how brave of you," said Diana, admiringly. "I couldn't possibly have done that."

Snubby went on with his tale of the night's doings; how he had looked through the locked kitchen door, and had had the idea of going to look in at the kitchen window clad in the bearskin, and had then gone out of the garden door and round to the window.

"There were boxes out there, piled up," said Snubby, "and the kitchen door was open wide."

"But I locked it!" said Mrs Tickle, amazed. "And what's more, I bolted it too!"

"Well, it was open," said Snubby. "Is it locked now?"

Barney went to look. "Yes, locked and bolted! They must have got in somewhere else, and opened the kitchen door from inside. And then, when they went, they must have locked and bolted it again on the inside, and gone out the way they came in."

"Probably a window somewhere. We'll take a look in a minute," said Roger. "Go on, Snubby."

Snubby told the rest of the tale. How he had been caught and how he had bolted down the cellar steps to escape the men, who had promptly locked him in.

"The box I saw them carrying up the

cellar steps must have been the last one," he said. "There aren't any more boxes like it down there. I had a look. My word, it was cold in the night; I was lucky to find an old mattress to sleep on."

It really was an extraordinary tale. Nobody knew quite what to make of it. So many peculiar things had happened since they had been at Rat-a-Tat House, but this last one, of boxes hidden in the cellar, and taken away in the middle of the night was the most puzzling of all.

"I suppose all the peculiar things fit together somehow," said Barney, when at last they were in the sitting-room having breakfast, with Snubby now dressed and comfortably warm again. "But the question is – how?"

"Yes, how does Mr No One, banging on our door in the middle of the night, fit in with the somebody who watched us by the snow house one night?" said Roger.

"And how does the walking snowman fit in too?" wondered Diana. "Why should he wander about and look into the kitchen window, frightening Mrs Tickle out of her wits?"

"I rather think I know!" said Barney suddenly. "Yes, I'm beginning to see how all the happenings can fit together like pieces in a jigsaw."

"What do you mean?" said Roger.

"Don't talk to me for a bit while I think it out," said Barney, buttering a piece of toast. "It's just beginning to dawn on me."

Snubby was eating his fifth piece of toast, and was now feeling extremely pleased with himself and his adventure. He was even inclined to boast, but this the others would not allow.

"It wasn't very clever to hear a noise in the night and go down by yourself instead of waking me and asking me to come with you," said Roger. "If I'd been with you we might even have caught the men, locked them into the cellar in the same way that they locked you in! You never know."

"I think I've got it," announced Barney suddenly. "Yes, I think I begin to see things now."

"What? Tell us," said Diana eagerly.

"Well, listen. Coming down here was quite a sudden idea of my father's and grandmother's," said Barney. "To all intents and purposes the house was closed till next spring – shut up and empty. Well, along comes someone who wants a very, very good place to hide something – perhaps stolen goods, perhaps smuggled goods. I don't know—"

"And what could be better than an empty house which won't be visited for months," cried Roger. "Yes, go on, Barney."

"Right. They decide to bring their goods here, and probably plan to hide them in our cellar till it's safe to take them to wherever they want to," said Barney. "So they break in somewhere, or get a key that will unlock one of the doors, and one night they arrive here with car, or van, or lorry—"

"And carry those boxes I saw down into the cellar," said Snubby. "Gosh, yes! That's it. Meaning to collect them in their own good time! And they locked the cellar door and took away the key just in case anyone should come here to do a bit of cleaning and perhaps even pop down into the cellar, and discover what was hidden there."

"Exactly," said Barney. "It certainly was a splendid hiding place. No one would see the van or lorry arriving in this lonely spot, far from any other house – no one would see the boxes being unloaded and taken into the house – and no one would see them being taken away again when the right time came."

"And then suddenly we come and spoil all their plans," said Diana. "What a shock it must have been for them to hear that we had arrived to stay for a while. How do you suppose they heard?"

"Oh, probably someone in Boffame village told them," said Barney. "Or they may have come along to have a look to see if their hidden goods were all right, and discovered us here."

"And one of them spied on us in the snow house," cried Snubby. "And dropped his glove there."

"But I don't see how Mr No One, banging at the knocker, fits in," said Diana, puzzled. "Or the walking snowman that went and peeped in at Mrs Tickle's window last night. Somehow I don't think she made that up."

"She didn't," said Barney. "I'll tell you how I think Mr No One, the knocker, and the snowman all fit into the picture. I think they were meant to frighten us away – so that we would go off and leave the coast clear for them. They would be able to load up their lorry again, or whatever it was they used, and hide the goods somewhere else."

"Gosh!" said Snubby, lost in admiration at Barney's explanations. "You're right. Mr No One was simply one of those men – Jim or Stan – hammering away at the knocker to make us think it was the old legend coming true. I nearly did think it too – we were all scared to death."

"It's a wonder we didn't leave at once," said Diana. "Mrs Tickle would have loved to go, I know."

"Yes, but to the man's great annoyance, we still stuck here and they had to watch us tobogganing all day yesterday, instead of rejoicing to see us pack up and go."

"We couldn't go, anyway," said Roger. "Unless a car came to fetch us, and we couldn't get Barney's father over because the phone is out of order."

"They wouldn't know that," said Barney. "So they tried to scare us once more, by dressing up in a white sheet, or something like that, and stealing the snowman's hat, and then peering through the window at poor Mrs Tickle."

"No wonder she was scared," said Diana. "We all thought she made that up, or was mistaken, but she wasn't. Poor Mrs Tickle! How awful to see the snowman peering through the window, hat and all."

"And when we still didn't get in a panic last night, I suppose they gave up trying to scare us and decided to get the boxes out in the middle of the night, hoping we wouldn't hear, and hide them in a safer place," said Barney. "But old Snubby heard them, and rather messed up their plans."

"But not enough to ruin them," said Roger. "They've got the stuff away all right, that's clear. I wonder what it was."

"I think we ought to try and find out," said Barney. "This may be something pretty serious, you know. If only we could phone my father! I wonder how long it will be before the telephone wires are mended."

"Ages, I expect," said Diana. "What do you plan to do now, Barney?"

"I plan to follow the tracks the men made carrying those boxes away," said Barney. "They'll show easily over the snow."

"Well, we'll have to buck up then," said Roger. "Look, the sky's full of snow and it's beginning to fall already. Any tracks will soon be covered."

"What I want to know is how Mr No One made tracks to the front door, and got away without leaving another set," said Snubby. "Who'll tell me that?"

Nobody bothered to answer him. They were all rushing to get their hats and coats to go and find the tracks the men made when they took away those big heavy boxes.

18

On the Trail

Diana stayed behind to tell Mrs Tickle a little of what Barney had said, and to carry out some of the dirty dishes. Mrs Tickle, looking astonished, tried to follow all that Diana was saying, but she soon gave it up.

"All I know is, there's some very funny goings-on here," she said. "And I don't like it. If the phone was all right, I'd phone Mr Martin and tell him it's dangerous to stay here and get him to fetch us. Knockings in the night, and wandering snowmen, and Snubby locked in the cellar! It just isn't right."

"Never mind, Mrs Tickle," said Diana, comfortingly. "I don't think we'll have any more 'funny goings-on' now – if Barney's right in what he says. So you needn't be scared, or carry your rolling-pin about with you."

"Indeed I shall – it goes with me wher-ever I go," declared Mrs Tickle, brandishing it. "Upstairs and downstairs."

"And in my lady's chamber," said Diana, with a laugh. "All right, you do what you want to do, Mrs Tickle. I think you've been marvellous." And with that she went out to join the others. They were examining the snow house, and the place where the snow-man had once stood.

"Look, Di," said Barney, as she came up. "The snowman has simply been knocked down and trodden on. The only things left are his two feet."

"And someone's broken down the back wall of the snow house," said Roger. "Walked into it, probably, or leaned on it when he was watching us through the window."

"*And* we've found out how Mr No One walked through the snow to the front door, and apparently didn't go back again," said Snubby. "I worked that out, actually."

"Oh, the clever boy!" said Diana, amused at Snubby's boasting. "How did Mr No One do it?"

"Well, watch. I'll go to that tree through the snow, and come back, and you'll only see one set of prints," said Snubby, "and all going one way!"

"Go on, then, show me," said Diana dis-believingly. Snubby grinned. He walked slowly to the tree, making well-defined foot-marks in the snow – and then, when he reached the tree, he stopped. He looked carefully over his shoulder to see the last footmark he had made, and put his foot in it; then the other foot into the neat print, and the next.

"He's walking backwards, and putting his feet into the same footmarks he's already made," said Diana, astonished. "What an idea!"

"Yes. So there *is* only one set of footprints all going to the tree, though Snubby has gone there and back," said Roger, as Snubby arrived back beside Diana again, grinning all over his freckled face.

"And that's how our Mr No One managed to puzzle us, when he walked up to our front door in the middle of the night, and hammered on it, and apparently didn't go back again," said Barney. "He just walked backwards in the prints he had already made."

"It was clever of you to find that out, Snubby," said Diana. "I never thought of that. I say, it's snowing quite hard. Have you looked yet to see if you can follow the tracks the men made when they carried off the boxes?"

"No, we'll go and do that now," said Barney. "If we don't the tracks will be covered. Let's take our toboggans with us, then we can do a bit of sliding down hills again. Skating's no good at the present moment."

But when they got to the outdoor shed

where the toboggans were kept, they had a great shock. The toboggans were not there!

"Blast!" said Barney. "Who's taken those?"

"Stan and Jim, I bet," said Snubby, feeling quite brilliant. "*And* I know what for."

The others stared at him. "You don't mean – you don't mean they've taken them to drag away those boxes," said Roger. "Oh, goodness! I hope you're not right."

But Snubby was right. When they made their way to the back door, outside which he had seen the big boxes set ready to take away, they found the toboggan tracks deeply indented in the snow there.

"Look – here's one set – and another," said Barney. "The runners of the toboggans have cut right down into the snow, almost to the ground."

"Yes. That's because the boxes were so heavy," said Snubby. "I bet those men saw our toboggans out in the shed there when they were snooping round, and one of them suddenly had the bright idea of using them to carry away the boxes. They'd be far too heavy to carry between them for any distance."

"Snubby's quite a detective," said Roger, half in earnest and half joking. "Get away, Loony; you're spoiling the tracks we're following. Go and play with Miranda."

But Miranda didn't want to play with

Loony. She was sitting on Barney's shoulder, trying to catch the snowflakes as they floated down round her. She couldn't make out why they disappeared as soon as they caught them.

"Let's see if we can follow the tracks now," said Barney. "They may go to that boat-house – you never know. They'll be easy to follow, because the men can't have taken all of the boxes at once on the toboggans – not more than two at a time, I should think – so they'd have to come to and fro a good many times, and make quite a track over the snow."

"Well, the tracks are beginning to go already," said Diana. "The snow is falling so thickly. Look, they go right round the house. Come on, let's follow them."

They began to follow the deeply-rutted tracks made by their toboggans. Snubby was feeling quite worried in case they would not find the toboggans; he had been so much looking forward to some more fun on them. Blast those men! What silly tricks would they be up to next?

The tracks led around the house and down the drive and then out of the gate. They led across the road and over the bank beside the pond. Then they led round the pond to where the boat-house was.

"There you are! We *thought* those men might have made the boat-house the next

hiding place for the boxes," said Barney, pleased.

"I'm surprised they didn't realise we could easily follow their tracks," said Roger.

"Well, they probably knew a heavy fall of snow was coming, and they hoped the tracks would be hidden," said Barney.

"Look – there's the boat-house. Let's go carefully in case the men are there."

So they went very carefully indeed, not talking or laughing, and not allowing Loony to bark even a small bark. The boat-house loomed up, all white, with a new layer of snow on the roof.

The toboggan tracks, still deeply indented in the snow, led right round the boat-house to the front of it, where the lake itself began. There the tracks stopped.

"It looks as if the men brought the boxes here, and unloaded them into the boat-house," said Barney, in a low voice. "I wonder where our toboggans are?"

"Look! Is that them over there?" cried Snubby suddenly. "Loony, go and look."

Loony leaped over the snow to where the newly-fallen snow was half covering something brightly coloured. He scraped at it and barked loudly as the children walked towards the snow-covered heap.

"Yes, it *is* our toboggans," said Diana. "They emptied them, and threw them into the snow, hoping they would soon be hidden. I hope they haven't damaged them."

The children pulled them out. No, they were quite all right, although the paint had worn off where the heavy boxes had scraped them.

"Well, that's something, at any rate!" said Diana thankfully. "I was afraid we might not find them again, and they're such beauties."

"What are we going to do next? Look in the boat-house?" said Snubby eagerly. "The men can't be there, or surely they would have yelled at us."

"Well, we can at least go and peep through that broken window," said Barney. "I wonder how the men got the boxes into the boat-house. I suppose they have a key to the big doors that open above water-level to let the boats out in the summer."

They went round the boat-house to the broken window. Barney looked boldly inside, but it was so dark in there that snowy morning that he could not make out even the outline of the boats. He felt for his torch, but he had left it behind.

"Blast!" he said. "Oh, you've got yours, Snubby – good." He flashed it quickly through the window, and all round the shed. There was no one there at all; at least, no one that he could see. "Empty!" he said. "Not a soul here. The men must have gone off, now that they have disposed of the boxes. I expect they think they've hidden them so well that no one will discover them. They don't know that we've spotted this old boat-house for a hiding place."

"Can you see the big boxes anywhere, Barney?" said Snubby, trying to peer in through the window too. "Let me look!"

"There's nothing to see in the way of boxes," said Barney. "But there wouldn't be. I expect they are under one of the boats, or covered with tarpaulins – sure to be, in fact. I bet they're here somewhere."

"Well, let's get in and look," said Roger. "We ought to be able to find them – it's not a very big place. Gosh, what a thrill to come across them! Do let's explore the boathouse, Barney. After all, it belongs to your family, so we won't be trespassing. Do let's."

19

Rather Disappointing

Barney did not need much persuading. As for Miranda, she didn't even wait for him to say yes. She leaped in through the broken window and bounded here and there, looking at this and that with great interest.

Barney began to break away the few remaining bits of broken glass in the window. "Very sharp edges!" he explained. "I don't want any of us to get bad cuts. Diana, you be very careful. Roger will help you up and I'll help you down inside the boat-house."

"I don't see how we can cut ourselves," said Snubby, impatient at having to wait. "We're all wearing thick gloves and boots. Buck up, Barney!"

Barney leaped inside the boat-house, and then Roger helped Diana up, and Barney helped her down. Roger followed and then Loony was handed up, and, last of all, Snubby came.

The boat-house was very dark indeed, for

the daylight hardly penetrated through the dirty windows. And, in any case, it was a dark day with the sky full of snow; quite a different day from any they had had.

The children had two torches, and with them they began to look all over the boat-house. It was a typical place for keeping boats, full of all kinds of gear, ropes, tarpaulins and half-empty tins of paint. It smelled musty, and the boats were fast-locked in the ice. They had once floated in water there in the boat-house, but now their keels were no longer afloat, they were ice-bound. Barney quickly realised that there was no possible chance of finding any boxes under the boats. He set to work to look under the tarpaulins and sails that lay about here and there.

"I don't believe the boxes are here," said Diana, at last, tired of floundering about the dirty boat-shed without finding a single box.

"I'm beginning to think the same," said Barney, puzzled. "After all, Snubby said they were big ones, and there were a lot of them, and they just can't be here. We've hunted everywhere."

It was very disappointing indeed. "We followed the toboggan tracks here, where they ended, and yet we can't see any sign of the boxes," said Diana. "Could the men have hidden them anywhere under the snow, do you think?"

"Well, they could, I suppose," said Barney. "But even one box would need a big pile of snow to hide it, and a lot of boxes would certainly make quite a mountain under the snow. Still, we can look."

So the next thing they did was to flounder about in the thick snow round the boat-house. They felt sure that the men would not have carried such heavy boxes very far. Loony leaped about like a mad thing, not knowing what they were looking for, but hoping it might be something eatable. Miranda watched him from Barney's shoulder, wishing they could go home to the nice warm fire. She didn't like the snow that kept falling, falling, falling.

There were no boxes hidden anywhere round or about the boat-house. Snubby was most disappointed. What a waste of a morning! He was amazed when Barney said it was time to go back to lunch.

"Do you mean to say we've spent the whole morning looking for those beastly boxes?" he said, in disgust. "No tobogganing, no skating, not even a spot of snowballing. What a waste. Well, anyway, I'm at least going to have a slide on the pond."

"It's got a covering of snow now. You won't be able to slide properly," said Diana.

But Snubby was on the pond, making a little slide of his own. *Whoooosh!* He slid along quite well and then fell over and slid

the rest of the way on the seat of his trousers.

As he was turning over to get up, he felt something under his hand and grasped it. What was it? He looked to see and gave a little exclamation.

"A cigarette packet – like the one Barney found in the boat-house. One of the men must have thrown it away last night when he arrived at the boat-house with the toboggans."

He went back to the others and showed them the packet. "Same as before," he said. "The man must have chucked it away over the lake."

Barney took it to compare with the packet he had found in the boat-house. "Just the same," he said. "Hello, it's not empty. It's half-full! Look!"

He was right. "Wasteful fellow, throwing away cigarettes," said Snubby. "I shall really have to speak to Stan or Jim about it when I next see them!"

"Ass," said Roger. "I say, isn't it snowing fast! By the time we've had our lunch all tracks will have been covered with another fall of snow. It's a good thing we followed the toboggan tracks when we did."

"Not that it did us much good," said Diana. "We didn't find a sign of the boxes. I wonder where they can be. Well, I suppose they simply must be somewhere in the boat-house."

They were quite ravenous when they got back to Rat-a-Tat House. Mrs Tickle was looking out anxiously for them. "You're late," she said. "I began to think you'd got lost in the snow."

"Has Mr Icy-Cold been wandering about again, or Mr No One?" asked Snubby. "What – nobody been peeping in at your window? Life is getting dull for you, Mrs Tickle."

"Go on with you," said Mrs Tickle, giving Snubby a push. "You've got far too much to say. My word, how wet you are! You'll have to change your things before you sit down to your lunch."

"Oh, blow!" said Snubby. "There's such a nice smell coming from the kitchen. What is it, Mrs Tickle?"

"You go and get those wet things off," said Mrs Tickle. "And dry Loony too. What a mess he's in. Stop pouncing at my feet, Loony. Stop it, I say! And just you take one more of my dusters away and I'll put you in the dustbin."

Soon all the children were sitting down to hot vegetable soup. Miranda was given an apple and nibbled it daintily, sitting on Barney's shoulder. But when she came to the pips in the middle she was not so dainty. She picked them out with her tiny fingers and dropped them into Barney's soup.

"I don't know why we keep you and Loony," said Barney, fishing out the pips. "I really don't. Pests, both of you."

The monkey took hold of the lobe of Barney's ear, put her mouth close and chattered in a whispery voice. Barney listened gravely.

"All right. As you apologised so very nicely, I won't say anything more, Miranda."

Diana chuckled. It always amused her when Miranda whispered into Barney's ear, and Barney pretended to know exactly what the little monkey had said.

After rather a big meal, the children sat round the fire talking about the peculiar happenings of the last few days. There was no point in going out, for the snow was still falling, and they even had to switch on the light because the day was so dark.

Mrs Tickle came in to see what they planned to do. "Don't you go out again," she said. "You might easily get lost in this. I can hardly find my way from the back door to the dustbin."

They all laughed. "Mrs Tickle," said Snubby, "there's something worrying me. How are you going on for food? No trades-men can come here, and we certainly can't get to Boffame village now."

"That would worry Snubby, of course," said Diana. "Food is his biggest interest."

Mrs Tickle laughed. "You don't need to worry," she said. "I brought a car-load of things from Boffame village when I came. Old man Hurdie at the post office, he said we were in for more snow, and told me to take all the food I could. Things will keep fresh for a week. The bread's too stale to use now, though, except for toasting, so I'll bake some myself."

"Good idea," said Snubby, approvingly. "Shall I come and help you?"

"No thank you," said Mrs Tickle. "I

don't want you messing about with my bread. All you want to do is to go and poke your nose into my larder. Just like my Tom, you are."

"What's going to happen if this snow goes on and on, and we get even more snowed up?" wondered Roger.

"I don't quite know," said Barney. "I wish we could phone. I can't see that we can do anything except stay here till my father thinks it's time we came home, and somehow finds a means of transport."

"A large sleigh and a few husky dogs to pull it is what we really want," said Diana.

"Yes, a sleigh with bells on," said Snubby. "Jingle-jingle-jing—"

R-r-r-r-ring! Rr-r-r-r-ring!

A sudden, shrill noise made them all jump. Then Barney gave a shout and leaped to his feet.

"The telephone bell! The wires must have been mended. Now we can get on to someone and tell them about the extraordinary happenings here. Hello, hello?"

Everyone sat up eagerly. Yes, it was Barney's father, anxiously asking how they were all getting on.

"Fine, Dad, fine!" said Barney. "But, I say, Dad, listen. Some very peculiar things have been going on here . . . Yes, peculiar things, I said . . . What? . . . Yes, I'll tell you if you hang on. Actually I don't quite

174

know what we ought to do about them. Well, here goes . . ."

And Barney launched into the story of the last few days and all their strange happenings. What a tale it was!

20

The Telephone at Last!

Mrs Tickle came running eagerly when she heard the welcome sound of the telephone bell once more. She and the others stood round Barney while he told the curious tale of the happenings at Rat-a-Tat House.

Barney's father was astonished.

"But what *is* all this?" he said, his voice ringing clearly through the receiver, so that even the others could hear it. "Disturbances in the night – breaking into the house and taking things from the cellar. Why was it locked when you arrived? It never is! And whatever had these fellows got hidden down there? Barney, is there anything more to tell me?"

"Yes, but I've told you all the important things," said Barney. "Can you possibly come down here, Dad? We're pretty well snowed up, and I'm not sure if a car can get through now. Thank goodness the phone wires are mended."

"Yes, thank goodness," said his father.

"Your grandmother was so worried about you all that I really think she was planning to put on my old skis and ski over hill and dale to you."

"Good old Granny!" said Barney, proud of the old lady. "I wouldn't be surprised to see her arriving here on skis – or even on a sledge drawn by reindeer. But Dad, is it possible for a car to get through now, do you think?"

"No, we couldn't risk it," said his father. "Not today, at any rate, with more snow falling. We'd probably get stuck in a snow-drift and be marooned there for days. Why, some of the villages that are completely snowbound are having to be helped by heli-copters. They drop food down, as you know. By the way, you've got plenty, haven't you?"

"Oh, yes," said Barney. "Dad, are you going to tell the police? I don't know what is in those boxes they hid in the cellar here, but it's quite certain they couldn't have got them away far, because no van or lorry could move from here; so they must be hidden somewhere near, though goodness knows where."

"Yes, I thought that too," said his father. "I shall phone the police at once, and let you know what they say."

Everyone was very thankful that the tele-phone wires were mended again. It was a real relief to be in touch with the outer world now that such strange things were happening. Barney put down the receiver and smiled round at the others.

"My father's on the job now," he said. "We needn't worry at all."

"Well, I'm glad to hear that," said Mrs Tickle, as they all turned to go back to the warm sitting-room. As they went, Miranda lifted the receiver and pretended to chatter into the telephone just as Barney had done! Barney swung round at once.

"You little copycat," he said, snatching it from her paws and putting it back in place again. "Why we put up with you and Loony I really don't know."

Miranda scampered into the sitting-room and sat on the top of the bear's head, looking very comical. Then she pretended to whisper something into the bear's ear.

"That monkey – she's a real comedian!" said Mrs Tickle. "Well, Barney, I'm relieved to think your father knows everything. What's he going to do?"

"Tell the police," said Barney promptly. "But what they can do at the moment I don't know – nobody can get through the thick snowdrifts, Dad says."

"Anyway, the men are not likely to worry about us any more," said Diana. "They've got their goods, whatever they are, so we needn't expect any more rat-a-tatting, or snowmen wandering about."

"That's true," said Roger. "Anyway, I expect the men have gone off somewhere now they've hidden their boxes. It must have been very cold and uncomfortable sleeping in the boat-house."

"Well, they can't have gone far in this thick snow," said Barney, looking out of the window. "They're probably hiding in some outhouse or other, but I wonder what they do for food?"

"Don't forget that the cellar had plenty of tins on its shelves," said Snubby. "They could help themselves to those when they took the boxes."

"So they could," said Roger. "I never thought of that. And you know, we've never discovered yet how they came into the kitchen. We know they didn't come through the kitchen door, because Mrs Tickle locked and bolted it, so even if they had a key, they couldn't have opened it."

"I'm going to have a look," announced Snubby. "A little detective work! Come on, let's see who can find out how the men got in."

Mrs Tickle remembered that she had bread to make, and hurried back to her kitchen. The others began to go round the different rooms and try the windows to see if they were all closed and fastened.

"They're all well and truly shut, and

fastened tight," said Barney. "All the downstairs windows are, anyhow. I simply can't imag—"

He stopped as Mrs Tickle came running into the room looking excited.

"I've found out how they came in," she said. "Through the larder window! It hasn't got a very good catch, and they've forced it, so they could climb in. Then they shut it after they went and I never noticed that the catch was broken."

They all went to examine the broken catch. "Yes, you're right," said Snubby. "They got in this way. My word, what a big larder this is, Mrs Tickle. And, I say, look at that pie. When is that for?"

"You keep your fingers off my shelves," said Mrs Tickle. "And who said you could take that jam tart?"

Barney was glancing up at the top shelves. "I suppose nothing has been taken from here by the men, has it?" he asked. "They'd be glad of food now."

Mrs Tickle fetched a chair and stood on it to look at the shelves above her head. "I don't know exactly what was here," she said. "There were tins and bottles and packets which I didn't touch. And, yes, they've taken a few things. I can see the marks in the dust where tins or something stood. Yes, I think they took a few tins. Well, I never did!"

"Taking food off the shelves and boxes from the cellar. They'll be sleeping in our beds next," said Snubby. "You'd better look out, Mrs Tickle."

"I'm certainly going to look under my bed tonight – with a rolling-pin in my hand," said Mrs Tickle fiercely.

"We'll let Loony do that," said Snubby. "He'll simply love to go hunting under everyone's bed. Won't you, Loony?"

"Wuff!" said Loony, joyously, and tore up the stairs as if he meant to begin that very minute.

They all went back into the sitting-room, and gazed out of the window. What a change in the weather! No clear sky, no pale, clear sun, no view over the gleaming lake; only endless snowflakes falling from a leaden sky.

"I don't envy those men, Stan and Jim, wherever they are," said Snubby. "They must wish to goodness we'd never come down here. I bet they planned to shelter in Rat-a-Tat House if it got too cold in the boat-house."

"They probably hoped to remove those boxes by lorry sometime this week," said Barney. "Their plans have certainly been upset. I do wonder where they hid those heavy boxes. They can't be very far away. They could never carry them any distance."

"It's odd," said Roger. "They put them on our toboggans and dragged them down to the boat-house, then took them off the toboggans and hid them. But where?"

"I'm tired of thinking about it," said Diana. "Let's play a game. Let's have a jig-saw race. We've brought plenty, haven't we?"

"Yes," said Snubby. "I'll get four. They're in the cupboard."

Soon they were all sitting at the big round table, each with a box of jigsaw pieces. "Go!" said Roger, and they all emptied out their pieces quickly, and began to sort them at top speed.

"I always pick out the blue sky bits first," said Diana. "Snubby, you've dropped a piece on the floor already."

Miranda was a little nuisance when jigsaws were being done. She was fascinated by the tiny coloured pieces and longed to help.

"Don't, Miranda," said Snubby, exasperated. "That piece doesn't go there. Now you've knocked out another piece. Barney, put her on your shoulder."

But she wouldn't stop there, and Diana thought that the only sensible thing to do was to give the little monkey a jigsaw of her own to play with, so she fetched another from the cupboard.

Miranda was delighted and proud. She settled down on the table, her jigsaw pieces spread in front of her, and fiddled about with them, chattering in her little monkey voice. Mrs Tickle could hardly believe her eyes when she came in with the tea-tray later on, and saw her.

"Well, I never!" she said. "That monkey beats everything. Are you ready for tea – or shall I leave the tray here till you've finished?"

"I've won!" said Snubby, fitting in his last piece. "I'm first! What do I get? The biggest slice of chocolate cake, and more scones than anyone? I've won!"

And just then the telephone bell rang again. Ah, was that news from Barney's father?

21

Diana Has an Idea

Barney ran to the telephone at once. Had his father told the police? What had they planned?

"Hello!" he said. "Hello! . . . Yes, it's me, Barney, Dad . . . Yes, of course I'll listen carefully."

He stood with his ear glued to the receiver, nodding his head and saying "yes – oh, yes" now and again in an excited manner, his eyes sparkling. The others crowded round trying to hear what was being said, but Barney had clamped the receiver so close to his ear, in order not to miss a single word, that they could make out very little.

Snubby could hardly stand still, he wanted so badly to know what Barney's father was saying, and at last he heard Barney say goodbye.

"Right, Dad. I'll do all you say, you can depend on me. I'll tell Mrs Tickle too. I say, how very exciting! See you tomorrow. Goodbye!"

He put the receiver back and turned to the others, his eyes still shining.

"What did he say, what did he say?" Snubby almost shouted.

"I'll tell you. Come into the sitting-room," said Barney. "Mrs Tickle! Oh, there you are! You come too. I've got exciting news."

They all went into the sitting-room, Loony as excited as the rest, though he didn't know what about. Miranda jigged up and down on Barney's shoulder, a piece of jigsaw puzzle still in one tiny paw.

They all sat down, and Barney began:

"My father got in touch with the police and told them everything. The police were very interested indeed. My father thinks they know what is in the boxes, but they didn't tell him. They're coming down here tomorrow morning to investigate."

"Tomorrow – in this snow!" said Roger, looking out of the window where the snow was still falling gently. "No car would get through."

"They're coming by helicopter!" said Barney. "We've got to prepare a landing-place for them."

"Whew!" said Snubby. "This is exciting! How do we do that?"

"Well, there's a big lawn at the back of the house," said Barney. "Very big, and quite flat, of course. And we're to clear as large a space as we can in the middle of it, so that the helicopter won't land in deep snow."

"Let's go and begin now," said Snubby, leaping up, quite forgetting that it was almost dark.

"Ass," said Roger. "Shut up, and let Barney go on."

"We're to mark the landing place some-how," said Barney. "With dark cloths, or something."

"We can take down the navy-blue cur-tains upstairs," said Mrs Tickle at once, as excited as the rest. "We can clear a big square and lay the curtains all round it. If they're likely to blow away we can weight them down with something heavy – tins of food, or something like that."

"But how many people are coming?" said Diana. "I thought helicopters couldn't take many."

"Three people are coming," said Barney. "My father, an inspector of police, and a sergeant, I think, Dad said. It's the only way they can come, and the inspector says it's absolutely essential that they should get those boxes."

"What can be in them?" wondered Snubby, jigging up and down in his chair just like Miranda. "I say, isn't this exciting? I hope those men won't hear the helicopter coming."

"Dad says it doesn't matter if they do," said Barney. "He says they'll merely think it's been sent to drop food or to see if we're all right. Anyway, he says it's more important at the moment to find the boxes than the men."

"Whew!" said Snubby. "Let's have another hunt for them then. We know they can't be far away; they're too heavy to carry any distance."

"Well, we did look all round and about, and in the snow and in the boat-house," said Diana. "Honestly, I don't think the men could have carried them any distance at all, once they took them off the toboggan."

"No. That's quite true," said Barney thoughtfully. "I've puzzled about that too. We know quite well where the toboggan tracks ended – by the lakeside."

"I suppose," said Diana suddenly, "I suppose . . . No, it couldn't be that."

"Couldn't be what? What have you thought of?" said Barney at once.

"Well, we found that the toboggan tracks ended by the lakeside, and we found the toboggans themselves nearby in the snow," said Diana. "But it's quite possible, I suppose, for the men to have slid the toboggans across the lake, to the bank on the other side, and have hidden the boxes there. And then slid the toboggans all the way back to where we found them in the snow."

The others stared at her, taking in this new idea. Barney slapped his knee and made Miranda jump in surprise.

"Yes! Yes, it's not only possible, it's very, very likely. If you remember, the lake was free of snow that night. We'd been skating on it all day, and the toboggans would slide over it easily enough. And then the snow fell and hid any tracks made over the lake! Even a thin layer of snow would hide any cuts made by the runners of the toboggans as they slid over the ice, weighted down by the heavy boxes."

"And I've thought of something else," almost shouted Snubby, making Loony jump this time. "That cigarette packet I found some way out on the lake – with cigarettes still in it. It wasn't thrown there by the men, it was dropped by one of them as he pulled a toboggan along."

"Yes. That's right," said Roger, clapping Snubby on the back. "That puzzled me too. Now you've solved that little mystery, Snubby. Of course it was dropped, not thrown. I say, I wish it wasn't dark. We could go across the lake and hunt for hiding places somewhere on the opposite bank."

"Let's take our torches and go," said Snubby, jumping up and making Loony bark.

"No, certainly not," said Mrs Tickle at once. She had been listening to all this in astonishment, not uttering a word. But now she had her little say. "Going out into the thick snow at this time of night, when it's pitch dark and freezing cold – you'd all be lost, and frozen to death by the morning."

"Rubbish!" said Snubby, too excited to listen to reason. "I'm going. Come on, Barney."

"No, Snubby, Mrs Tickle's right," said Barney. "It would be a mad thing to do. We can easily wait till morning. We'll have to be up early. It will take us ages to clear the thick snow off the lawn, and make a square big enough for the helicopter to land in safety."

"We'll have to find some spades," said Diana.

"There are some in the garden shed," said Mrs Tickle. "We'll get them out tomorrow. Now, look, don't you want any tea? The buttered toast and the scones will all be cold."

"Gosh! I'd forgotten all about tea. However could I do that?" said Snubby, sounding most surprised. "Di, lay the cloth quick. I'll help to set out the things. Buttered toast all going cold. What a thing to happen!"

Mrs Tickle laughed and went back to the kitchen to get the tea she had made in the big brown teapot. That Snubby! Just like her Tom, he was, always hungry, always one

190

for a joke. She heard the patter of feet and looked round quickly. It was Loony, and even as she turned she saw him make off with her hearth-brush. By the time she had put down the kettle and teapot she was holding he had disappeared upstairs. Goodness knows where he would put that brush!

Tea was a most exciting meal, with everyone discussing helicopters, police, possible hiding places for the boxes on the other side of the lake, and where Stan and Jim, the two men could be.

"They might be with the boxes," said Snubby, putting cheese spread on to his fourth piece of toast. "They might have built themselves a snow house like ours, and have made a fine hide-out, with plenty of our tins for food, and snow for water."

"In that case we'd better go carefully," said Diana, alarmed. "I don't want to find those two men. Let the police do that. But I'd love to find the boxes."

"We'll take the toboggans with us when we go across the lake tomorrow," said Roger. "Then if we do find the boxes we can bring two back, one on each toboggan. Wouldn't the police be pleased to see them!"

They were not at all tired that night, for they had had too little exercise, and Mrs Tickle found it very difficult to get them to bed. She badly wanted to go herself, for she

had baked and cooked a good deal that day, and was tired. She peeped in at the sitting-room door at half past nine.

"Aren't you ready?" she said. "I'm going up to bed now. Please come quickly."

"Right," said Barney, hearing the tired note in Mrs Tickle's voice. "You go on up, Mrs Tickle. We're just coming. We'll knock at your door to tell you we're safely upstairs."

They talked for ten minutes more and

then went out into the hall, which was now in complete darkness.

"Don't turn out the light!" shouted Barney to Diana. "Now what's up? Surely, our Mr No One isn't up to his tricks again. It's pitch dark here in the hall. I'll just feel about for the light switch and see what's happening."

"Oh, dear!" said Diana. "Surely we're not going to have any upsets tonight! Buck up, Barney. Wait, I've got a torch. I'll shine it round the hall and see if anyone's about."

She shone it nervously round the dark hall. And yes – someone was hiding there. The beam fell on a small furry head, peeping out from behind the back of a chair, with two bright eyes gleaming mischievously.

"It's Miranda!" cried Snubby. "Oh, you little wretch! You turned out the light again, didn't you? Loony, get her!"

But before Loony could get near her the little monkey was bounding up the stairs in glee, chattering away in delight. Aha! She had played a trick that Loony would never even think of.

22

Here Comes the Helicopter

Next morning dawned clear and bright. The snow had ceased falling, and once again the sun shone from a clear, pale-blue sky. All the children were pleased, because this would make things much easier for the helicopter.

They were up nice and early, and gobbled their breakfast. Diana went to help Mrs Tickle with the washing-up, and the boys went to look for spades in the big garden shed not far from the kitchen. It was locked, but Mrs Tickle gave them the key. They unlocked it and looked round for spades.

"Good!" said Barney, as his eyes fell on quite a selection. "Big ones and little ones. Here, have this nice little one, Snubby."

"Don't be a fat-head," said Snubby, annoyed. "I'm as strong as you are – stronger, if anything."

Diana and Mrs Tickle came out to join them as they were arguing about the spades. Mrs Tickle chose a hefty spade. Barney looked at her admiringly. Whatever she did, she did very thoroughly.

They went to the lawn, their spades over their shoulders. The snow was quite thick and deep here – about half a metre, Barney thought. "Let's mark out a good-sized square," he said. "And begin to clear it at once."

They marked out the square, and then began to shovel away the snow vigorously. It was very hard work. Snubby began it much too vigorously and was forced to take a rest before the others did. "You should have taken the small spade as I told you," said Barney, his blue eyes twinkling.

They soon had quite a good piece of the middle of the square cleared. "It's big enough for a helicopter to land here now," said Roger, considering it carefully. "Though it would be a pretty near thing. Mrs Tickle, what about you and Diana going to get those dark curtains now, and we can lay them round the clear patch as soon as we hear the noise of the helicopter. We don't know when it will come, but we'll go on digging hard till it does."

Mrs Tickle and Diana disappeared indoors. They came out in half an hour with armfuls of dark curtains, taken down from the upstairs rooms.

They laid them down in a heap and again joined the boys in their digging. No helicopter arrived, and soon the diggers felt as if they simply must have another rest. Barney was digging in his shirt-sleeves now, and seriously considering working bare-backed, he was so hot.

Mrs Tickle went indoors and brought out some buns and ice-cold lemonade. Nobody wanted a hot drink just then! They ate and drank eagerly, for the exercise had made them very hungry and thirsty. Then they set to work again.

"It's a quarter to twelve," said Mrs Tickle, at last. "I think I'd better go in and make some soup, and peel potatoes, and so on. With three extra lunches, we'll need plenty of food. Diana, you come too; you've done plenty of digging."

"Yes, go and help Mrs Tickle," said Barney, who saw that Diana was getting tired. "We've not much more to do. There's a big clear place for the helicopter to land now."

Diana went in to help Mrs Tickle and the boys resumed their shovelling. Certainly they had made a big enough landing-place now. Barney felt quite proud of it.

Then, through the clear, frosty air, there came a distant throbbing. The boys looked up. It must be the helicopter.

"Quick! We must spread out the dark curtains!" shouted Barney, suddenly excited. "And don't you dare run off with any of them, Loony – or you either, Miranda!"

Mrs Tickle and Diana came running out as soon as they heard the helicopter, and helped to put the dark curtains all round the big, cleared square of lawn. They could now see the machine quite clearly – not a very big one – its rotor spinning above it.

It came nearer and nearer, and the noise grew louder. "It's coming down! It's seen our marked-out square!" shouted Snubby, in

intense excitement. "Here, helicopter, here; this way, this way!"

Carefully and gracefully the helicopter descended to the clearing. It came to earth with hardly a jerk, and the sergeant, who was piloting it, jumped out first. He grinned round at the excited children.

"Fine!" he said. "We saw our landing ground miles away. Splendid!"

Then came Barney's father, Mr Martin, and last of all the trim, burly inspector, with a grim mouth, but kind eyes twinkling under bushy brows.

"Well!" he said. "Good morning to you all. You've had a little excitement, I hear."

Mr Martin smiled round, glad to see everyone looking well and cheerful. "I'd never have let you come if I'd known you were going to be snow-bound like this," he said. "Come along – let's go into the house and talk."

Off they went, and Mrs Tickle became very busy indeed in the kitchen while the others filed into the sitting-room to exchange their news.

The inspector and the sergeant listened to everything with great interest, the sergeant taking notes all the time. The children had to tell the story over again right from the beginning. The inspector asked many questions, and was pleased with the clear, ready replies.

"Intelligent children, there," he said, turning to Mr Martin, who had sat silent, astonished once again at the strange story. He turned back to the children.

"Mr Martin says you tried to find the boxes, after the men had taken them away, but couldn't," he said. "Have you any idea at all where they could have been taken?"

"Yes, sir," said Snubby eagerly, and he told him of their latest idea – that the men had slid the toboggans across the lake, taking the boxes to the other side. "But the snow hid their tracks across," he said, "so we actually thought that they had taken the toboggans no farther than the boat-house; we never thought of them going across the frozen lake. And I found a half-full packet of cigarettes out on the lake, too; they must have dropped it there on their way across."

Now the inspector and sergeant were sitting up straight. "Ah!" said the inspector, "now this is something. It's obvious that the men couldn't carry the boxes far, so . . ."

"Sir, what's in the boxes, do you think?" asked Snubby, longing to know.

"We'll have to wait and see," said the inspector, tantalisingly. "If it's what we hope it is, we shall be very, very pleased."

Mrs Tickle appeared in the doorway. "I hope I don't interrupt, gentlemen," she said politely, "but I've got a meal all ready to bring in, if you'd like it now. Or I'll keep it hot for you if you need to go on talking."

"No, no – we'll have it now, Mrs Tickle," said Mr Martin at once. "Very good of you to think of it. Have you much more questioning to do, Inspector?"

"None," said the inspector, and the sergeant snapped the elastic band round his black notebook and put his pencil away. "But we'll do a little searching this afternoon, if you children would like to show me the lake and the boat-house and all the rest. We may be able to find those boxes."

"Oh, good," said Snubby, rubbing his hands. "I say, things are getting pretty exciting, aren't they?"

"Very," said the inspector, smiling at the red-haired, freckled boy with the spaniel at his heels.

"I'll go and help Mrs Tickle," said Diana, and Roger went too. Miranda leaped off Barney's shoulder and scampered out of the door as well, much to the astonishment of the two policemen.

"She's gone to help herself to something she fancies," said Barney, grinning. "She's probably lifting the lids off the dishes to see what's inside."

Mrs Tickle had provided a very good lunch indeed and stayed in the room to help to serve such a large company. The two policemen stopped being rather ponderous and sharp-eyed, and joked and laughed as cheerfully as Mr Martin did. Altogether it was a most enjoyable meal, especially for Loony, who was provided with an astonishing amount of scraps under the table.

Miranda was thrilled, because besides a big steamed jam sponge pudding, there was a dish of pineapple and cream, and Barney had to keep his eyes on her. She loved pineapple and would help herself out of the dish whenever she thought there was nobody looking.

"And now," said the inspector, having thoroughly enjoyed the lunch and the company too, "we will all go out and you will show me the boat-house, and anything else I need to see. Then we will trek across the frozen lake to the other side, and see if we can find where those boxes are hidden."

All was excitement immediately. The four children rushed to get their coats and scarves while the three men waited for them.

Soon they were all ready, with Loony rushing about more madly than usual, holding a small duster in his mouth, and defying everyone's efforts at getting it from him. Miranda waited her chance and dropped down on his back as he rushed past. In anger and surprise Loony turned on her and barked, and the duster dropped from his mouth.

In a second Miranda had it in her paw, and was up on Barney's shoulder again, stuffing it down his neck for safety.

"What a pair!" said the inspector, chuckling. "As bad as a couple of children." Everyone laughed – and then out of the house they went, stopping to show the inspector the enormous lion's head knocker on the front door.

"Hmm. Those fellows badly wanted you out of the house, didn't they?" said the inspector, eyeing the knocker. "Well, come along; we've got a lot of work to do this afternoon."

23

Snubby Stubs his Toe

The children took the three men down to the boat-house first of all, and showed them the broken window there, and the place where the toboggan tracks had ended.

"And that's where we found the toboggans, over there, almost hidden by the snow," said Snubby, pointing.

The policemen went into the boat-house and searched for a while, saying very little. They came back and shook their heads.

"Impossible to hide anything much there," said the inspector. "But there's no doubt the men hid there, by the number of cigarette ends. Now, let's go across the lake. Scrape the snow away a bit here and there, in case we find any tracks on the ice underneath."

They scraped here and there but could find no tracks of the toboggan runners. They reached the other side of the lake and began a systematic search. The inspector allotted searching spots to each of them. The drifts of snow were high in places, and it was just possible that the boxes might have been hidden there.

It was tiring work, stamping in the drifts and searching in the snow for anything hard, such as a box. They soon exhausted the spots the inspector had allotted and went farther afield, but here the snow lay perfectly smooth and unbroken, and it was fairly obvious that no big boxes were hidden there, or the snow would have lain unevenly.

"Well, we don't seem to be very successful, do we?" said Mr Martin, disappointed. "We've pretty well examined the whole of this bank of the lake. The rest of it has bushes growing down to the edge, and it's unlikely the men would go there."

"I think we'd better give up for this afternoon," said the inspector. "I don't imagine that the men will try to retrieve their boxes while it's so difficult to get transport, such as a lorry, to take them away by road. Wherever they are, those boxes will have to remain hidden till the roads are clear of snow. Then the men will lose no time in collecting them from their hiding-place and getting them away one night."

"Right," said Mr Martin. "We'll go back to Rat-a-Tat House for tea then. Dusk is coming quickly now and we can hardly see what we're doing."

They turned to go back across the lake. The weather had turned warmer, and in places the snow was now melting fast. They came to the lake and stepped on to it to go back to the boat-house.

Mr Martin and the two policemen went first, talking together. Snubby and Loony came last, shuffling through the snow that lay on the frozen surface.

Snubby suddenly stubbed his foot against something hard and gave a yell of pain.

"What's up?" said Barney.

"I've stubbed my toe," said Snubby, standing on one foot and holding the other. "Oooh, I felt it right through my rubber boot!"

"Don't make such a fuss," said Barney. "Just a bit of frozen snow, that's all."

"It was not," said Snubby, indignantly, and immediately began to hunt for whatever it was he had stubbed his toe on. He soon found it and uncovered it.

"Here, look, Barney!" he shouted. "It's a great piece of solid ice. Look! Not a bit of frozen snow. No wonder it hurt my toe."

Barney turned back impatiently, and looked at the piece of ice Snubby had uncovered. It was rather curious – large, circular and thick, and lay flat on the frozen surface of the pond. Barney stared at it in surprise.

"Why is it round like that?" he said. "What a peculiar piece of ice." He looked at it more closely and then gave a yell that startled Snubby considerably.

"Hey, Dad! Inspector! Come back here a minute – quick!"

Snubby stared at Barney as if he had gone mad, and Loony rushed round in circles, barking loudly as he always did if there was any excitement about. Mr Martin and the two policemen turned in surprise and made their way back as quickly as they could. "What is it?" said the inspector. "Have you found something?"

"Yes, this piece of ice," said Barney. "Look – perfectly round, and quite large. It's been sawn out of the icy surface of the pond."

"Ah! Now we're getting warm," said the inspector, and knelt to examine the circle of ice. "Perfectly round – done with a saw, of course, as you say. But why? Aha! This is very interesting. What a pity it's getting so dark! Let me see, now. Could you boys run back to the house and get torches and some spades to shovel away the snow just here on the ice? We must see where this circle was sawn from."

Tremendously excited, the four children raced back to the house, grabbed torches, found spades, and raced out again, hardly bothering to reply to Mrs Tickle's astonished questions.

Torches shone on to the snow near where Snubby had found the piece of round ice.

Shovels were used vigorously to shovel away the snow round about.

"We'd better be careful not to fall into the hole made when this piece of ice was cut out," said Roger.

"No fear of that," said Mr Martin. "The water below would have frozen again almost immediately."

In under five minutes there came a yell from Barney. "I've found the place, this must be it. Look!"

They went to him, and shone their torches at his feet. There, uncovered by the snow was a circle of ice clearly defined on the surface of the pond, showing where a round piece had been removed, and where the water had frozen again.

"It looks rather like one of those round drain-covers you see in the road," said Diana. "Goodness! Do you think – do you possibly think – that the men shoved the boxes down under the ice, knowing it would freeze again and hide them safely?"

"Looks like it," said the inspector grimly, peering down at the new circle of ice, so neatly filling in the place where the first one had been removed. "What an ingenious idea! Stan and Jim are evidently men with brains."

"What shall we do, sir?" asked the sergeant, with great interest. "It's getting very dark."

"I think we can safely leave things till tomorrow," said the inspector. "The men are not likely to try to remove the boxes from the lake until the weather is good enough to arrange for a lorry to collect them. We'll be along here tomorrow and have a little excitement sawing out another piece of ice ourselves, and probing down into the water below."

Everyone felt very excited, but rather disappointed that they would have to wait till the next day. "I shan't sleep tonight for thinking of it," said Snubby. "Sir, we could do it all right now, surely. I'll get a saw, and we've got torches."

"Ass!" said Roger. The inspector didn't even bother to reply to Snubby. He led the way to Rat-a-Tat House, feeling very pleased. Nobody took any notice of the way Snubby limped, and he felt cross. If he hadn't found that big round piece of ice, nobody would ever have found that most ingenious hiding-place. He thought they might at least sympathise with him over his sore toe.

Mrs Tickle had to hear the news of course, and was surprised and excited.

"To think of that now," she said. "Making a hole in the ice and dropping the boxes down. What a thing to do! Well I must say those men are full of ideas. What with hammering at the knocker in the

middle of the night to scare us away, and pretending to be the snowman walking around! I'll be glad when you've got them safely under lock and key, Inspector."

"So shall I," said the inspector grimly. "Very glad indeed. Of course, we don't know for certain that we shall find the boxes down there, nor what they contain. But I'm hoping – yes, I'm certainly hoping."

"Fancy having to wait a whole night before we find out," complained Snubby bitterly. "Loony, what about you and me slipping off at midnight and finding out for ourselves? Are you game?"

Loony was game for anything, of course, and said so, but the inspector did not approve of such fantastic suggestions.

"Nobody is to go near the lake again until the sergeant and I go tomorrow morning," he announced. "We will all have a nice quiet evening, and look forward to some good luck tomorrow."

Certainly the evening passed pleasantly enough, for the inspector proved to have a fund of astonishingly interesting stories. Snubby listened open-mouthed to the ways of the police in tackling crime.

"My word!" he said, in awe, as the inspector described the capture of a particularly clever spy. "I'm never going to do anything wrong, never. Nobody has any chance at all against people like you, Inspector. I think I'll join the police force when I grow up. Loony would be awfully good at tracking thieves, I bet he would."

"He's just tracked down another of Mrs Tickle's brushes," said Diana. "Look – it's her hearth-brush again. Loony, have you no interests in life besides brushes and dusters?"

Loony deposited the brush at Snubby's feet as if he were bringing him a really fine bone. Snubby frowned at him.

"Idiot! Here am I praising you up to the inspector and you do a silly thing like this. Take it back at once, and apologise to Mrs Tickle. Quick, before Miranda gets it!"

Mr Martin laughed. Snubby always amused him. "Time you went to bed," he said. "Remember, we may have some difficult work to do tomorrow."

24

The End of the Mystery

Snubby was up first the next morning, with Loony racing round his feet. Mrs Tickle came downstairs a few minutes after Snubby, and found him trying to rake out the sitting-room fire and light it for her.

"I couldn't sleep a minute longer," he explained. "I can't think why the inspector isn't up. Surely it is his duty to get on with this job as soon as possible?"

"You're a caution, you are," said Mrs Tickle. "Leave that fire alone, now. You've made ten times more mess than I do. Go and wake the others, because breakfast is to be earlier than usual."

"Thank goodness for that," said Snubby, and went back upstairs with Loony at his heels.

Breakfast that morning seemed a waste of time to the four children – even to Snubby, who liked a very big one, and could always be counted on to finish up the last piece of toast. But today he was as impatient as the others to get back on the frozen lake.

At last, armed with two saws and some thick rope, the little party set off to the lake. Miranda was on Barney's shoulder and Loony was finding that now the snow had melted on the lake, the surface was slippery again, and his legs slid away in all directions, making him feel most ridiculous.

They came to where they had discovered the newly-frozen circle of ice on the lake; close beside it was the loose piece on which Snubby had stubbed his toe. The inspector nodded to the sergeant, who knelt down and tried to insert the end of the bigger saw into the ice.

It wasn't easy, but at last the saw was really working, and the sergeant was puffing and panting as he sawed round the frozen circle. At last it was done – the circle was complete.

The sergeant inserted a wedge and heaved up the piece of ice he had sawed round. Up it came, and he deposited it beside the first one. Everyone peered down into the icy water.

"I can see something," said the sergeant, his head almost in the hole. "I can just about reach it, sir, I think."

He put his arm down into the water and groped about. His hand felt a rope and he pulled at it. Up it came and he dragged it out of the hole.

"It's fastened to something down below, sir," he said, tugging at it. "We'll have to heave hard I'm afraid."

"Tie that rope to ours," said the inspector. "Double ours to make it strong. Come away from that hole, lad – you'll fall in."

Snubby removed himself in disappointment. The sergeant knotted the two ropes together, and then he and the inspector did a little heaving.

"Something's coming up," panted the sergeant, pleased. "Whoa – steady, here she comes! Anyone else like to help pull? It's very heavy."

The edge of a box now showed through the big hole – then the top of it. And with another heave the big box came right over the edge of the hole and slid along the ice. The sergeant promptly fell over backwards, much to Loony's joy.

Everyone gazed at the box. "Yes," said Snubby joyfully. "That's one of the boxes the men took out of the cellar. Hurrah!"

"Shall I open it now, sir?" asked the sergeant, getting up carefully. The inspector nodded, whereupon the sergeant produced a most interesting collection of tools in a leather case. How Snubby wished he had a set like that.

With a great deal of care and manipulation, the sergeant at last got the lid open, and the children stared down inside. The

box had been quite watertight, apparently, for there was no moisture inside. Something gleamed up brightly as the children bent over to look.

"Guns!" said Snubby, in awe. "I say, look at those guns!"

The inspector and the sergeant looked at one another and nodded. Yes, this was what they had been hoping for and expecting. Mr Martin nodded too.

"Good work!" he said. "Let's hope we've got all the guns down there that those fellows stole from the army camp. I suppose they were going to be shipped out of the country secretly, and used against us some-where."

"I say! Mrs Tickle won't like the idea of having had dozens of guns stored in her cellar," said Snubby. "She's really scared of them. Are we going to get up the whole lot? Look – there's a rope hanging down from this one, into the water. Is it tied to the next box? Are they all tied to one another?"

"Shut up, chatterbox," said Barney, eager to catch every word said by the three men. This was a serious business – traitor's business!

A thought struck him. Traitor's business, that rang a bell in his mind. Yes – what was that old legend? The knocker, the lion's head knocker, was never sounded unless there was a traitor in Rat-a-Tat House! And there was a traitor when that knocker sounded – it was sounded by the traitor himself. Barney made up his mind to tell the others this idea as soon as he got them alone. Very, very curious!

"Fetch your toboggan, lad," said the inspector to Snubby. "We'll drag this box back to the house for further examination. As for the other boxes, we'll leave them till I can get men down here to look at them. Their contents are probably exactly the same as this."

Snubby sped off and brought back his toboggan. They lifted the heavy box on to it and Snubby and Roger dragged it over the slippery ice. What a find!

"What about the other boxes, sir? Suppose the thieves come and get them!" said Snubby.

"They won't come until the snow has gone and they can get a lorry down the roads," said the inspector. "And a few men to help them."

"But aren't you going to set a watch, sir?" said Snubby. "I mean, you don't know when they might come."

"The first lorry that gets through to this district will be watched," said the inspector good-humouredly. "And just in case you think we don't know our business, I can tell you that as soon as the lorry is loaded with the guns, and the men drive off, it will be stopped, searched and driven off to the nearest police station. Does this meet with your approval?"

"Oh, sir!" said Snubby, actually blushing. "I know you know your business – I just thought – well, those men may come along and get those boxes out, and—"

"But don't you think it is a good idea to let them drag them out, and load them into the lorry, so that we haven't anything to do but drive it to the police station?" said the inspector. "Or would you like to take on the job of getting them out yourself?"

"Oh no, sir," said Snubby. "I – er – well

– er – er . . ." And he dried up completely, annoyed at being laughed at by the burly inspector.

The inspector and the sergeant, with the box of guns, took off in their helicopter after lunch. The children were sorry to see them go – everything had been so very exciting! They waved till the helicopter was a speck in the sky and then went indoors.

"Dad, are you going to stay on with us?" said Barney, delighted to have his father with them.

"Yes, I thought I would," said Mr Martin, smiling. "If I shan't spoil the party."

"Oh, no," said Diana, who liked Barney's father very much. "We'd love to have you. I'm sorry the snow is going, though – there won't be much more tobogganing or snow-balling but there'll still be skating."

"My father skates marvellously," said Barney, with the note of pride that was always in his voice when he spoke of his father. "Dad, isn't Dick coming after all? Didn't his cold get better?"

"Yes, but there wasn't room in the helicopter for him too," said Mr Martin. "So it will be just me and the rest of you."

"Good!" said Barney, pleased. "Jolly good! I wonder if we'll still be here when those men come to get their guns from the lake. I do hope so."

"Yes, I expect we shall," said his father.

"That will be another bit of excitement to round off a most exciting holiday. My word, fancy your coming down here for a bit of winter sport just when the men had hidden their stolen guns in our cellars. What a shock it must have been for them to see lights in the house all of a sudden."

"Snubby really solved most of the mystery," said Diana generously. "If it hadn't been for him things wouldn't have turned out so well."

"You're right!" said Snubby, beaming. "I heard the noise in the night and went down and found the boxes . . ."

"I bet it was Loony who growled or something," said Roger. "And don't forget that you managed to get yourself well and truly locked up."

"And it was Snubby who knocked his toe against that round piece of ice and made us realise where it came from and set us on the track of the guns," went on Diana. "Yes, and it was Snubby who found that cigarette packet half full of cigarettes."

"I fact, we might almost say that Snubby solved the mystery of Rat-a-Tat House!" said Mr Martin, smiling at Snubby's delighted face. "He deserves a reward. Anything you'd particularly like, Snubby?"

"Yes," said Snubby at once. "There's something I badly want to do – can I do it?"

"What is it?" asked Mr Martin cautiously.

"I want to go and bang that lion's head knocker on the door," said Snubby. "Crash it down, like Mr No One did that night. You've no idea what it sounds like, Mr Martin."

"Ass," said Barney. "Let him do it, Dad. He won't be happy till he does bang that knocker. Little things please little minds you know."

"That knocker is an enormous thing," said Snubby indignantly. "Come on, Loony – let's go and have a bash."

"Tell Mrs Tickle what you're going to do, for goodness sake," called Diana, "or she'll go up in smoke. And Barney, hang on to Miranda. Look she's up on the mantelpiece with her Snap cards again, bless her!"

Snubby went to the front door and opened it, Loony at his heels. "Loony," said Snubby solemnly, "I and I alone, solved the Rat-a-Tat Mystery – and we're telling the world we did it. Stand ready!"

He lifted the huge knocker with both hands and then hammered with all his might on the door.

Rat-a-tat-tat! Rat-a-tat-tat! Rat-a-tat-tat!

All right Snubby, we heard you. Now do go and sit down and be quiet!